THE WITCH WHO SETTLED THE ACCOUNT

PIXIE POINT BAY BOOK 1

EMMA BELMONT

EMMA ONLINE

Emma loves hearing from her readers!

You can contact her at the links below.

Website: emmabelmont.com

Newsletter: emmabelmont.com/newsletter

Thanks!

1

If Maris Seaver could have ordered perfect weather, it would have been like today's. The sun blazed bright in an ultramarine sky while a soft, salty breeze wafted in from the nearby bay. As she strode across the quaint Towne Plaza, she marveled yet again at the charming climate and matching surroundings. To her delight and some relief, Pixie Point Bay had changed little since she'd been a child.

The Victorian buildings of the downtown area had been nicely maintained, their pastel colors radiant in the afternoon light. Even the grass of the plaza seemed freshly trimmed. Of the many places around the world where she had worked, from the beach resorts of Thailand to the alpine retreats of the Colorado Rockies, she'd never found anything to compare to the west coast's Middle Kingdom, particularly this town. Apparently the residents felt that the more things remained the same, the better they were, and she agreed. Despite the unfortunate circumstances that had brought her back, she was glad to be here.

Pixie Point Bay was home.

She was just approaching the red Oriental gazebo in the center of the plaza when its occupant turned to her.

"Maris? Maris Seaver, is that you?"

Millicent Leclair was what Maris's aunt had called the busiest busybody in the world. In her early eighties, she was the president of By Hook or Crook, the town's crochet society. She and Aunt Glenda had known each other almost their entire lives. Millicent was exceptionally spry, with immaculately-groomed gray curls and the attitude of someone who would never die. For all Maris knew, she wouldn't.

"Millicent," Maris said, approaching the old woman. She stood in the shade of the gazebo, looking particularly small under the large structure, but with an enormous handbag slung over her shoulder. "What are you doing this fine afternoon?"

"Just watching the world go by," Millicent replied. "You can learn a lot from people-watching, you know. I just had the loveliest chat with Robbie Grayson. He's working on another model plane. Good with his hands, that one." She pinned Maris with her black eyes. "How are the B&B and lighthouse?"

"The lighthouse," Maris said, smiling like a proud parent, "has yet to miss a day of operation. And the B&B is, I'm happy to report, as busy as ever."

It was a question that Maris was getting used to answering. When Aunt Glenda had died suddenly of a heart attack, Maris had inherited not only the Victorian Bed & Breakfast and attached lighthouse, but also the roles of lightkeeper and B&B owner. With Cookie's help—the B&B's chef for the past few decades—Maris felt she had settled in quite nicely. The townsfolk were naturally curious, of course, and had all been supportive. But it wasn't lost on Maris that the B&B and lighthouse were a tourist draw for the entire region. Many of the local businesses depended, at least to some extent, on hers.

"Good news indeed," Millicent said nodding crisply. She paused and seemed to look all over Maris. "Pixie Point Bay looks as though it's been good for you. At the moment, though, you have the look of a woman on a mission."

Maris chuckled. "I suppose you could say that. Errands won't run themselves."

"So true," the other woman replied noncommittally. Then her eyes twinkled. "Are you planning on staying in Pixie Point Bay?"

This question was relatively new but Maris had known the answer for some time. After twenty-five years in the grinding hospitality industry, moving from one troubled hotel to another, and living out of her suitcase, the answer had been clear from the start. Although Maris had originally started in boutique hotel settings with an aim to provide gracious hospitality to weary travelers, she'd become one herself. By the time she'd arrived back in Pixie Point Bay, she was carrying too much extra weight, had a divorce under her belt, and was suffering from burnout at the age of fifty.

"Yes," she said, emphatically, "I'll be staying."

Millicent bobbed her head. "Well, I'm glad to hear it. That lighthouse is important, bed and breakfast or not. I'm glad to know it will be staying in the Seaver family." There was a pause, and she added, "It certainly must feel like a change of pace, though, coming all the way here from the big city."

"You know," Maris said, "not as much as you might think. I know that my Aunt's death was sudden, but..." She shrugged. "It feels like, since coming here and taking over the B&B, that everything's sort of fallen into place. Is that a bad thing to say?"

Millicent sniffed, thought for a moment, and shook her head. "I don't think so. Sometimes it takes a new perspective to figure out what's missing in your life."

"Exactly," agreed Maris.

"Well, since you're here for good," Millicent said, "you really should join By Hook or Crook. It doesn't matter if you don't know how to crochet. We'll teach you, and the ladies and I have been itching for a new member for a while now."

Maris smiled, wondering how many other townspeople Millicent had tried to recruit for the club. "I actually do know how to crochet," she replied, leaving out the fact that the last scarf she made had looked like something her cat had shredded—and that was before he'd actually gotten his paws on it. Nonetheless, the idea of joining the club was appealing. Who knew? With practice, she might even become decent. "I'd love to visit sometime."

Millicent smiled, the gears turning behind her bright eyes. The old woman was making a mental note of everything Maris said, no doubt to be brought up later with the other club members. Still, there was something else in Millicent's expression, something more perceptive than just the look of an old busybody.

I should ask Cookie if Millicent is one of the magic folk.

If anyone would know, Cookie would. She had been the one to break the news to Maris that, not only her aunt, but Maris herself were descended from a long line of witches, as was Cookie.

There was just something about Millicent that said there was more to her than met the eye.

"So what is this errand you're on, Maris?" Millicent asked, still watching her.

"I'm actually on my way to the credit union," Maris replied, glancing toward the building in question. "I think it's about time I opened an account."

As if she'd gotten a taste of something sour, Millicent's mouth turned down, her eyes darkening. She turned to look toward the credit union, brow furrowing, and gave an almost imperceptible shake of the head. Her whole demeanor had changed in an instant, from lighthearted to indignant. Maris opened her mouth to ask her what was wrong, but Millicent cut her off with a brisk, "Have a nice day." The older woman turned on her heel with astonishing speed. Before Maris could respond, she was already leaving the gazebo, her footsteps echoing on the concrete as she stomped away.

Maris blinked and stared after her. What in the world had gotten into the older woman? She'd already marched nearly halfway across the plaza. Sensing it would do no good to call out after her, Maris could only watch for another few moments before she shrugged. She would have to get to the bottom of that another time.

Without running into any other curious neighbors, Maris made it to the credit union in just a few minutes. Like most of the rest of the plaza buildings, it was a Victorian nestled on a grass lawn set back from the sidewalk. If fact, it looked more like someone's home than what one would usually expect for a bank. Pulling open the antique blue door, Maris found herself in what looked like a renovated parlor with three massive oak desks—two in front and one at the back. The name plaques on the front ones identified the people behind them as tellers, although there was no glass barrier separating them from the customers.

"Welcome to the Pixie Point Bay Credit Union," said a young woman, a petite brunette with glasses. She was standing and looking through a cabinet. According to her name plate, she ewas Ashley Pound.

Maris smiled at her, taking another step into the room, and said, "I was hoping to open up an account."

"You'll want to speak with Mr. Martin for

that," Ashley replied, indicating the desk in the back.

Seated behind it was a large, balding man with a goatee and round glasses. He hunched over a stack of papers with his back to the corner of the room. The plaque on his desk read, "Edwin Martin - Manager."

The man looked up when he heard his name, his beady eyes fixing on Maris, and a moment later a smarmy smile spread across his face. "I can take care of you here," he said, gesturing at the chair across from him.

Maris took a seat, holding out her hand. "My name is Maris Seaver," she said. "I'm new to town."

Edwin sized her up before taking her hand and giving it a lazy shake. His fingers were warm and sweaty.

"I've heard about you, Ms. Seaver. Yes, I have." Turning to the other teller, a blonde girl who couldn't have been much over twenty-five, he snapped his fingers and said, "Jessica, go get the fruit bowl in the back. We don't want a new client going hungry, do we?"

Ashley, the brunette, glanced at him. "Do you want me to do it, Mr. Martin?" she asked.

"I'm already up, and I think Jessica is in the middle of–"

"No," Edwin answered, his tone curt. "Jessica can do it." Snapping his fingers again, he pointed at the door to another room. "Jessica. Now, please."

The blonde opened her mouth to speak, seemingly thought better of it, and stood up, looking resigned. Satisfied, Edwin turned back to Maris. "Now," he said, "Ms. ... What did you say your name was?"

"Maris," she replied. "Maris Seav–"

"Do you want some coffee, Maris? I was thinking of having a cup, myself."

Even if she hadn't already had her caffeine fix for the day, the way he ordered the tellers around rankled her. Hoping to spare the women any more busywork, she said, "I'm fine. It's a little late in the day for–"

"Jessica," bellowed Edwin, "bring two coffees while you're at it! And don't forget the sugar and creamer!" Maris pressed her lips together. Edwin Martin might make a good banker but his people skills were adding up to a big zero. She was about to steer the conversation back to the matter at hand when Edwin said, "You're the one who took over the B&B, right? Cute place. Never stayed there myself."

She inclined her head. "My aunt left it to me."

"Interesting idea, having it connected to a lighthouse. Makes it hard to value though, being so unique."

"Well, I'm not particularly in the market to–"

"Finally," Edwin said, and she turned to see Jessica emerging from the back room, carrying a silver tray.

On it was an ornate china bowl filled to the brim with grapes, apricots, plums, and cherries, which the teller set down between the two of them. Her movements stiff, she shifted saucers and coffee cups to the desk. She reminded Maris of someone who was being made to touch something dirty, keeping as much distance between herself and Edwin's desk as possible. She was practically stretching just to set the china down while avoiding eye contact.

Edwin either didn't notice or didn't care, and poured an ample amount of cream into his coffee, along with a small mountain of sugar. He raised his eyebrows, holding the bowl out for Maris, but she shook her head, thinking about the weight she needed to shed.

Edwin shrugged. "Suit yourself." Reaching out with a plump hand, he plucked a handful of grapes out of the bowl and began to shovel them into his mouth. "So," he said between bites, "what kind of account do you want to open?"

"A savings account, I think."

He swallowed and took another grape. "If you're not planning to move your funds around any time soon, I'd recommend share certificates. They're like CDs, but the interest rate is higher than a normal savings account. I would–" He coughed, cleared his throat, and continued. "That's my advice, at any rate. Here." He rummaged in a drawer for a moment, producing a brochure. "Take a look."

As Maris glanced down at it, Edwin began to cough again, spluttering like there was something in his throat.

"Mr. Martin, are you–" she began, but he held up a finger.

"Yes," he said between dry hacks. "Fine. I'm just going to get some water." Still coughing, he pushed back from the desk—no small feat for someone his size—and retreated in the direction of the back room.

Maris was left to look over the brochure, which was mostly fine print, but had trouble concentrating as Edwin's coughs continued from the other room. There was the sound of water running, and the hacking kept up, seeming to grow more harsh even after he paused to take a drink. She could hear him sputtering, and then, all of a sudden, there was the sound of something—a piece of furniture maybe—toppling over. Then glass shattered, followed by a loud, meaty thump. Maris's head snapped up and she looked at the two tellers, who were still in their seats, eyes wide as they looked from her to each other.

Without thinking, she sprang to her feet and hurried in the direction of the sound. "Mr. Martin?" she called. "Are you all right in there?"

Rushing down a short hall, Maris pushed through a half-open door and found herself in a brightly lit kitchen. For a moment she stood in the doorway, confused, before her eyes drifted downward and her hand flew to her mouth.

Edwin Martin was sprawled face-up on the kitchen floor, his mouth open but completely slack. His glassy eyes stared at nothing. She dashed to his side, knelt, and pressed two fingers to his neck—no pulse. Staring at his unmoving chest, she tried again but the result was the same. She sat back on her heels as an icy cold sank into her stomach.

The man was dead.

2

———

By the time Maris had gotten over the initial shock, it had been too late to prevent the two younger women from coming in. Struggling to her feet, Maris turned to them, their faces white.

"Jessica," Maris said to her as she blocked her view. "Call 911." The blonde teller blinked once, then again. "Jessica," Maris said, gently taking her arm and turning her toward the door. "911. Please."

Without looking back, the young woman left and Maris heard her run back to the front room.

"I'll call Dr. Rossi," Ashley said, pointedly averting her gaze. "His clinic is just across the plaza."

"Thank you," Maris said, touching her

shoulder, and then hurried from the room with her.

While Jessica gave the 911 dispatcher the address, Ashley called the doctor. The two conversations took place side by side, Ashley finishing first, as the emergency dispatcher kept Jessica on the phone.

Ashley glanced back down the hallway. "What happened?" she whispered.

Just as Jessica hung up, the front door flew open and Dr. Rossi ran into the credit union. Slim, middle-aged, and wearing a white doctor's coat that matched his hair, he was carrying a medical kit.

"What's going on?" he asked, looking from one woman to the next.

"It's...it's Mr. Martin," Jessica said, her voice cracking. "He's..." She turned to Maris.

"I think he's dead," Maris said, her mouth suddenly dry. "He was coughing and couldn't seem to stop, and when he went to the kitchen to get water, there was a crash. I went in and...found him on the floor."

"Okay," said the doctor. "Okay. Stay here. Which way is the kitchen?" Ashley pointed, and he ran past them down the hallway.

As far as Maris knew, Rossi was the only

doctor in Pixie Point Bay. For a town with so few residents, there wasn't really a need for more. In emergencies, the hospital in Cheeseman Village, to the north, was within striking distance.

As the three of them waited, Jessica couldn't seem to stand still. The tall blonde shifted her weight uneasily from one foot to the other. Ashley, the shorter brunette, pushed her glasses up her nose, hugged herself, and stared at the hallway. Maris couldn't help but think of the cemetery on the hill overlooking the town. She'd visited her aunt's grave there only last week. As she imagined another plot being dug, she shuddered and closed her eyes.

In just a few minutes the doctor returned. He set down his kit and addressed Maris. "I'm afraid you were right. Edwin Martin is dead."

Jessica gasped a little, and Ashley slowly shook her head. Maris had that sinking feeling again, and swallowed hard.

The doctor extended his hand to her. "I'm Alfonso Rossi."

"Maris Seaver," she said, shaking his hand.

"You say he was coughing?" he asked,

looking from her to the two younger women. Although Ashley was still holding herself around the middle and Jessica had gone pale, they both nodded.

When he turned back to her, Maris agreed. "He'd been eating grapes by the handful. I think he might have choked."

For a moment, the doctor looked confused. But when he seemed about to reply, the front door banged open and a young man stumbled into the credit union. His brown hair was tousled, and his expression grim. Even without the apron from the Main Street Market, Maris thought she recognized him— a cashier perhaps or one of the kids who bagged groceries.

"What's going on?" he demanded, eyes wide. "Where's my dad?" His voice was unsteady as he approached the doctor. "The boss told me you called. He said it was an emergency."

"He's in the kitchen, Bryan," the doctor replied, taking a step toward him, "but–"

Bryan tried to sidestep him, but Dr. Rossi put a hand on his shoulder. "I don't think that's a good idea, son. I'm afraid he's died."

Bryan angrily shook him off and pushed

past him, disappearing down the hall. Although Rossi started to go after the boy, Maris quickly said to him, "He might need a moment alone." The doctor paused in mid-step and then turned back to them.

"I can't believe this," Ashley said, shaking her head and putting a hand to her chest. "Was it a heart attack? Was that it? I mean, I know he was overweight, but..."

"We won't know for sure until a thorough examination can be done," Dr. Rossi replied. "Did somebody call the police?"

"I did," Jessica said. She was trembling now, looking thinner than ever. "They said they would send someone. That was a few minutes ago, so hopefully they'll be here soon." She glanced at Maris. "Do you...do you really think he choked?"

"I don't know," Maris replied. "That was just a guess."

Bryan re-emerged into the front room, his complexion a sickly gray. His face was flat and emotionless, and even from a distance it was clear he'd broken out in a shivering sweat.

"Bryan," Maris said, "are you okay?"

He shook his head, his lips pressed together in a thin line as he hurried past them. "I'm going to be sick." He crossed to one of the bathrooms and disappeared inside.

"I was afraid of that," Dr. Rossi murmured, and they all went silent.

After a few moments, the toilet flushed and Bryan emerged, looking as though he was on the verge of keeling over.

"Why don't you sit down, Bryan," the doctor said.

The poor boy's in shock, Maris thought, and rolled one of the teller's chairs over to him.

He stared at her for a moment, swallowed, and nodded, sinking into the chair. Jessica opened a nearby cabinet and withdrew a bottle of water, which she handed to him. He gave her a grateful look but said nothing as he accepted it.

Maris turned to Ashley. "Do you have any more of those?"

She went to the cabinet and extracted another three bottles. She passed one to Maris but the doctor declined his. She set it down, kept the other for herself, twisted off the cap and took a long swig. She didn't seem to be doing much better than Bryan, and Maris couldn't blame her.

She took a good drink as well, regretting now that she'd left the B&B without a proper lunch. The water seemed to hit her empty stomach and roil around. Even so, she took another swallow. She knew it would be important to stay hydrated.

In her many years at hotels and resorts all over the world, Maris had seen her share of emergencies—and even been part of a few. But there were two things that they all shared in common: they brought out the best and worst in people, and they were inevitably followed by many questions. In the strange lull, she took a moment to take in her surroundings. She noted the people, the room, its furnishings and objects, committing everything to memory.

The wailing sound of a siren in the distance made them all look to the door.

3

———

Maris headed out onto the porch just as the boxy red ambulance pulled up, lights still whirling. Following it was a white SUV with the Medio County sheriff's orange and green markings, a vehicle that Maris recognized. It had been Sheriff Daniel "Mac" McKenna who had investigated her aunt's death—in what seemed like a lifetime ago.

Though the EMTs moved briskly with their equipment, it was clear that they knew they weren't here to rescue someone living. As the two tellers joined her outside, Ashley held the door for the paramedics. "The doctor is inside," she said.

"Maris," Mac said, as he ascended to the porch. His gray eyes settled on her and he raised his eyebrows. "I didn't expect to see you here—not that I'm complaining. It's good to see you."

Just the sound of his familiar voice and his assured manner put her more at ease. "You too, Sheriff," Maris said. "Although I wish it were under different circumstances."

"We certainly agree on that," Mac said, glancing over her shoulder, then back at her. "Are you okay?"

She nodded. "A little shaken up, but I'm guessing we all are." Taking a step to the side, she gestured to the open door. "Mr. Martin is in the kitchen. We haven't moved the body."

"Thank you," he said, giving her a smile before he turned and followed after the paramedics.

"I can't believe this is happening," Jessica said, running a hand through her long blonde hair. She was sweating, although the air conditioning had been running inside. "He's dead. I mean, he's really, actually..." She shook her head. "I can't believe it."

Ashley put a steadying hand on her arm. "This has been some shift. I would say we should go home for the day, but they're probably going to want to talk to us." Turning to

Maris, she asked, "What do you think we should do?"

Glancing out towards the street, Maris saw a small crowd of townspeople already beginning to form, having either seen or heard the ambulance, or caught wind of the emergency somehow.

"The authorities are most definitely going to have questions for us," she said, eyeing the plaza. Though she'd adore staying outside in the fresh air, it wouldn't be long before the gathering crowd had questions too. "I think it's time to go back inside." Maris opened the door for them. Ashley gave her a pained look and headed back in, with Jessica following close behind. It was going to be a long afternoon.

Once they were inside, Maris shut the door. Ashley took a moment to hang the "Closed" sign in the front window.

"Good thinking," Maris said. The last thing they needed was someone coming in to deposit a check while there was a body being examined.

The voices of the sheriff and the EMTs came from the kitchen. Bryan exited the bathroom and went immediately to flop down in the teller's chair, putting his head in his hands. He'd probably been sick again. Dr. Rossi paced in front of Edwin's desk, rubbing his chin and shaking his head periodically as if in the middle of a debate with himself.

"What is it, Doctor?" Maris asked, as Jessica and Ashley both found a seat.

Dr. Rossi gave a start, but then rubbed his chin again. "Nothing. Just thinking." There was a pause before he looked at the two tellers and asked, "Had Mr. Martin gone whale watching recently? Before today, I mean."

Jessica frowned, thought for a moment, and then shook her head. "I...I don't think so. At least he didn't mention it."

"He couldn't have gone whale watching," Ashley said, leaning on her desk with her elbows. "The season hasn't started yet. It goes from December to June."

"Hmm." Dr. Rossi pressed his lips together, his brow furrowing, but he didn't elaborate.

There were footsteps in the hall and all eyes turned that way. Mac emerged into the front room, his face impassive.

"The paramedics confirmed it," he announced. "Not that I doubted your word, Dr. Rossi," he continued, turning to him, "but it's protocol to double-check. Did you notice anything unusual in your examination?"

"I don't want to step on the coroner's toes," Dr. Rossi said.

"No worries there. The coroner will have the final word. Just your professional opinion."

Dr. Rossi looked from Maris to the doorway to the kitchen, and then back to Mac. "It looked like choking to me. Something cut off his airway, that's for sure."

"Maybe the grapes," Maris said, feeling like a broken record.

Mac raised his eyebrows, turning to her. "Grapes?"

Maris nodded. "He was eating grapes right before his coughing fit started. Maybe something went down the wrong pipe."

"Okay," Mac said. "I'll pass that along to the coroner." He turned to face Bryan, who was still sagging in his chair, looking stunned. He hadn't moved or spoken since the authorities had arrived, but his face seemed to be slowly returning to a less gray color, which Maris took as a good sign. Mac approached the boy slowly, stooping a little to look at him as he said, "Bryan, you should head home. People will be in touch with you shortly to make arrangements, but for now, just try to get some rest, okay? You've had a rough day."

Bryan swallowed, raising his head to look at the sheriff, and nodded robotically. "Okay," he said, his voice cracking. "Yeah. Okay." His movements leaden, he pushed himself out of his chair, wobbling a little on his feet. Mac steadied him with a grip on his elbow.

"Do you need a ride home?" Mac asked.

"No," Bryan said, his voice sounding far away. "I'll be fine. I ride a bike."

He shuffled to the exit but paused, glancing back toward the kitchen. Then he pulled open the door and stepped out into the afternoon sun. Through the window Maris could see the small crowd of onlookers part for him to pass. A few people patted him softly on the shoulder.

"Dr. Rossi," Mac said, "you're free to leave, too. I'd just ask that you don't discuss this too much with the townspeople. The less said the better."

"Understood," Dr. Rossi said. "I'd better

be getting back to the clinic. My nurse doesn't like me taking too long on house calls. See you later, Sheriff. Let me know if you need anything else."

"Thank you, Doctor," Mac said, as Rossi gathered his things and left the same way Bryan had.

This time, however, the gathered towns-people seemed to crowd closer. She could see him saying a word or two, and then their shocked looks as their eyes shot back to the credit union, and then to each other.

The paramedics emerged from the kitchen. "Sheriff," said the one in the lead, "we'd like to take the body now, if that's all right."

"By all means," Mac said, indicating the back of the credit union. "Can you bring the ambulance around the back when you re-move him?"

"Sure thing," the EMT said. "Is there an alley back there?"

Ashley stood. "Yes, and a back door where we take deliveries. I'll show you." One EMT went with her and one exited to the front. Moments later Maris could hear the ambu-lance start up, as Ashley returned.

"Thank you," Mac said to her. Then he addressed the three of them. "I'm going to need to ask you all some questions." Jessica sighed and slumped forward. "I'll keep it as brief as possible."

The back door opened and they all heard the bone chilling sound of the metal gurney rattling into the kitchen. Maris shivered a little.

"Jessica," Mac said, "I'd like to start with you." The sound of the wheeled stretcher retreated and the back door closed. "Maris and Ashley," he continued, "would you mind waiting outside?"

Maris heard the doors on the ambulance close and the engine start up. Of course, there was no siren. She gestured for Ashley to precede her. "We'll be on the porch," she replied.

4

With the departure of the ambulance, Maris was relieved to see that the onlookers had dispersed as well. She and Ashley sat on the steps of the porch. For a few moments they simply sat in silence. No one traversed the plaza, and only two cars drove past. For all the world, it looked like any other day.

The water had settled her stomach and now Maris hoped that it wouldn't start growling. She couldn't help but look at her car where she knew there were three candy bars squirreled away. It hadn't been intentional *exactly*. She'd bought them in an airport on the trip home from Hong Kong and forgotten about them. A week ago, when she'd been looking for the rental car agreement, she'd run across them.

Maris heard Ashley sigh and looked over to see her pinching the bridge of her nose. "What is it?" Maris asked.

"I'm going to have to balance the cash drawer," she said, "and all the numbers really. Deposits, withdrawals. Everything." She blew out a breath.

It already felt like it'd been a day and a half. "How long will it take?" Maris asked.

"Honestly," Ashley said, glancing over her shoulder, "it'll probably go quicker than it usually does. Mr. Martin would have Jessica order dinner delivered. I'd have to wait until he was finished eating before I helped him with the closing."

Maris glanced up toward the sun, which had begun its descent toward the ocean. "Well, at least it's an early day of sorts."

"True," Ashley agreed.

The door behind them opened and Jessica emerged, her eyes red and a purse slung over her shoulder. She glanced at Ashley. "He wants to talk to you next," she said, not pausing. Although Maris glanced up at her to say goodbye, Jessica walked passed her without noticing. "I'm out of here."

"See you tomorrow," Ashley called after her, and Jessica waved a hand in the air without turning. Ashley got up and gave Maris a tired smile. "Hope it's just as quick for me."

"Fingers crossed," Maris agreed. "I'll hold down the porch while you're gone."

Mac hadn't lied when he said it wouldn't take long. Within minutes Ashley was emerging from the credit union and waving Maris in. "Your turn."

Maris got up, and dusted off her skirt. "I'll try to be just as quick." She turned and re-entered the building for what seemed like the twentieth time that day.

Mac was sitting at Ashley's desk, scribbling in a notepad as he scratched his chin. He looked up when Maris closed the door, smiling a little when she approached. "Thank you again for staying," he said as she sat down. "I know this probably isn't what you had planned today."

"At least the company is good," Maris said, smiling a little, and the sheriff smiled in return. "So what do you want to know?" she asked, watching as he flipped to a clean page and wrote her name down.

"Why don't you start with when you arrived," Mac said, his pen poised over the paper.

"Okay," Maris said, casting her mind back over the afternoon's events. "I got here maybe ninety minutes ago, give or take. I was coming to open a savings account. Edwin seemed fine. I mean, he was a little short with the tellers, but there didn't seem to be anything wrong with him." Mac nodded, and she continued, "We sat at his desk over in the back, and he had Jessica get us some coffee. She brought cream and sugar, as well as that bowl of fruit." She pointed in the direction of Edwin's desk, where the coffee, now cold, sat next to the intricate china bowl. "Edwin ate a bunch of grapes."

Mac frowned a bit as he glanced at the desk. "You said that before as well."

"Yes. Why?"

He turned back to her. "It's just that there are no grapes in that bowl."

Maris's eyes narrowed as she peered around him. He was right. Where before there had sat a giant bunch of red grapes, bigger than Maris had ever seen, now there was a spot that was suspiciously barren. Apricots aplenty, along with cherries and plums, but there was not a single grape to be seen.

"That's odd," she said, frowning. "I can swear there were grapes there. Edwin was eating them by the handful."

"Are you sure?" Mac asked. "Could it have been something else?"

Maris pursed her lips. No, it could not have been something else. Of that she was sure.

Mac glanced over at the fruit bowl again, and she took the opportunity to discreetly move her fingers to her temple, giving it a couple of firm taps, aware that the gesture might come off as strange. The image of the fruit bowl returned to her, like seeing a photograph. Edwin had shoveled the red grapes into his mouth like a starving man.

Maris had been in high school when she'd realized that the other students weren't able to recall information at will. But only in college had she heard the term photographic memory. Of course what Maris never said about her 'excellent memory' was how it made if difficult to forget the incident in the elevator.

"Maris?" Mac asked, turning to look at her. "Are you all right?"

"Yes," she said, coming back to the present. She gave him a firm nod. "Yes. There were definitely grapes in the bowl. No doubt in my mind." When he didn't reply, she added, "There were two ample bunches of them, closest to him in the bowl. Closer to me were the apricots. I recall four. In between were the cherries and plums. I'd guess about a dozen cherries, none of which he ate. And I think you'll find three plums—quite ripe if I'm not mistaken."

Mac's eyebrows went up. "I rather doubt you are." He made a few notes on the pad, then he fiddled with his pen for a moment. "Maybe he ate them all."

"No," she said firmly, "there were plenty left when he went back to the kitchen."

Mac glanced over his shoulder to the back of the house. "Maybe someone put them back in the fridge."

"It's worth a look," Maris said, and the two of them got up and went to the kitchen. Maris hesitated just inside the threshold but now that the body was gone, it seemed like a sunny kitchen in a Victorian house.

Mac followed her gaze to the floor. "Man's inhumanity to man makes countless others mourn," he said, one hand on his utility belt and looking suddenly tired.

"What was that?" Maris asked, turning to him. It had the sound of something classical.

He met her gaze with his gray eyes. "Robert Burns," he replied. "My favorite poet. He always seems to have the right words."

"It's beautiful," Maris said. She paused for a moment and then added, "And quite apt."

"I'm glad you think so," Mac said, before turning to the refrigerator. Maris watched as he pulled open the stainless steel door. She peered over his shoulder as they both scanned the inside. There was plenty of food, fruit included, but no grapes to be seen.

"That's odd," she said, straightening as Mac stood back up.

"Agreed," he said, still staring into the interior. "Edwin Martin's death was likely an accident, or possibly a heart attack, but it never hurts to play it on the safe side."

As Maris watched, he fetched a trash bag from under the sink and unloaded everything from the refrigerator into it: cans of soda, the remainder of the fruit, and some containers of leftovers, which he double bagged. In the freezer there were only trays of ice cubes. Out in the main room, he used a different trash bag and put the contents of the fruit bowl in it.

"While I don't think there's any reason to have forensics pay a visit," he said, making a final note before tucking the small notepad in his breast pocket, "I don't like the way the food remains don't match your obviously superb memory." He headed to the front door.

"That's probably a good idea," Maris said, grabbing her purse and holding the door open for him so he could step onto the porch. She followed him back outside.

Ashley, who had been leaning against the railing, went to the door. "I'm just going to fetch my purse and lock up. I'll do the balancing and numbers tomorrow, since I guess I'll have to be here early to open."

"I guess you'll be handling things for a while," Maris said, sorry for the extra burden on the young woman.

Ashley shrugged. "It's not like Mr. Martin

did any real work, anyway." She sighed and went back inside.

"Is there anything else you need from me, Sheriff?" Maris asked when they reached the sidewalk.

He shook his head. "Not for now. Thank you, Maris. You've been a great help."

"You're welcome," she replied, smiling, even though she wasn't sure how true that statement was.

Ashley exited, locked the front door, and passed them as she headed to her car. "I need a warm bath and some serious snacks in bed tonight." She waved to them.

"Sounds like a plan," Maris said, waving back to her, as Mac put the bags of food in his SUV.

He closed the door. "I'll meet with the coroner," he said, running a hand through his salt and pepper hair. His eyes crinkled at the edges as he gave her another one of his empathetic smiles, and Maris couldn't help but smile back. There was a moment of silence and he looked like he was debating something. Though he opened his mouth as if to ask her a question, he closed it again and cleared his throat. "See you later, Maris."

"See you later, Mac," she replied. He gave her a cordial wave out the window as he started up the car, and then he was gone down the street, the sound of the engine fading.

As Maris made her way across the Towne Plaza, she passed the red gazebo in the middle and thought back to Millicent's sudden change in demeanor when she'd told her she was on her way to the credit union. The way she had looked at the place struck her as doubly odd now, like it was tainted somehow, or poisoned.

Millicent Leclair's home, where she hosted the By Hook or Crook Crochet Club, was just up ahead. Idly Maris wondered if the woman was there, watching the goings-on. No doubt she already knew what had happened to the credit union manager. Glancing up at the upstairs window, Maris saw a curtain suddenly come down. She smiled a little to herself and continued to where she had parked her rental car. No doubt Millicent knew more than she did.

As Maris settled into the driver's seat, she stretched her neck, trying to relieve some of the achy stress. But as she did, her empty stomach finally gurgled loudly in protest. She stared at the glove compartment for a good three seconds before she leaned over, opened it, and took out the candy bars. She left two on the passenger seat, and quickly opened the third. It looked none the worse for its storage time so she bit into the chocolate-covered, caramel, peanuts and nougat, and had to sigh. It was everything she'd remembered: sweetness, creaminess, and just the right amount of crunch.

"So good," she muttered around a mouthful, just as her neck popped. She tilted her head from side to side, and got another couple of cracks. Before starting the engine, she took another, smaller bite.

I'll just have half, she thought. *That'll be enough to get me home.*

Although her hollow insides were feeling better as she backed the car up, Maris couldn't shake a nagging feeling that there was more to Edwin Martin's death than she'd seen.

And she still didn't have a credit union account.

5

Maris drove her small compact over the familiar, manicured gravel of the B&B's long driveway. The tires crunched to a stop as she steered the vehicle into one of the empty parking slots.

With a single grab, she picked up the three empty candy bar wrappers and stuffed them in her purse. The last thing she needed was for someone to see the remains of her precipitous fall off the diet wagon.

Beyond the grand and gabled two-story Victorian and the towering lighthouse just behind it, the sun was sinking toward a thin layer of iridescent clouds at the horizon. Maris got out and gazed up at the conical white tower, its beacon whirling in the dusky light. The sunset had bathed its flank in tones of rose gold.

"That color looks good on you, Old Girl," Maris said quietly.

The moist sea breeze carried the scent of ocean spray from the rocks below the point, as well as the briny scent of seaweed. Maris let it wash over her as she closed the car door and ascended the steps of the front porch.

The interior of the grand Victorian home matched the outside, as though time had stood still. But as Maris passed the finely appointed front parlor, library, living room, and dining room, it wasn't the period furnishings and decor that occupied her mind. She was already thinking about the evening wine and cheeseboard, affectionately known in the hospitality trade as the Wine Down.

In the kitchen, Maris went directly to the gleaming, stainless, industrial refrigerator. Like the rest of the B&B, the room's decor was quaintly comfortable and in keeping with the period, but the appliances were all modern. Aunt Glenda had made sure that Cookie, the B&B's chef for decades, hadn't lacked for any modern convenience. From the double ovens to the six burner stovetop, extra wide broiler, oversize microwave, and double sinks, it was a kitchen that meant business.

"Let's see what we've got to work with," Maris said to herself, as she pulled open the heavy door.

As usual, she was on her own for the Wine Down. She and Cookie had fallen into their routine almost immediately. While the chef took care of the gourmet breakfast buffet, and the guests were on their own for lunch and dinner, Maris created the sumptuous spread for the evening wine and cheese.

As she surveyed the various artisanal varieties from Cheeseman Village, she let her creativity take over. Unlike the many hoteliers that she'd worked with over the years, Maris didn't care for set formulas when it came to wine and cheese pairings. As she called up an image of the bottles available in the dining room's wine cabinet, she compared it to the cheeses and fruits.

A tiny, tinny, harmonica-like meow, drew her attention to the floor.

"Hello, Mojo," she said to the fluffy black cat swirling around her ankles. "Come to help me pick?"

Her aunt had named the little guy after a famous blues harmonica player, George "Mojo" Buford. Whether his namesake was as friendly, Maris didn't know. But the peculiar sound of his voice made the name only too fitting.

He stopped circling and looked up at her with his big orange eyes. Then he sat down and stared into the refrigerator.

Maris tilted her head at him. If she didn't know better, she'd have sworn he understood her. "Well?" she asked.

He gave his signature meow again, sounding exactly like a little metal instrument.

"I see," she said. "I'm afraid that's not much help."

But as he began to lick one paw, a plan gelled in her mind. The pungent and crumbly bleu cheese would make the perfect foil for their locally bottled port wine, with its thick body and sweetness. Then, as a contrast, the saltiness of a hard parmesan would go nicely with a bubbly but dry Prosecco. As a bonus, those were both Italian.

She took everything to the dining room's sideboard, including the cheeseboard itself, where she would slice and assemble. This was a reception technique that she'd stumbled upon by accident. Instead of getting everything ready in the kitchen and bringing it out as a *fait accompli*, she found that guests liked to observe, nibble a little as she sliced, and chat.

First, though, she popped the cork on the Prosecco, opened the port, and filled a decanter with fresh cranberry juice. She set these beside the wine glasses, and then fetched a selection of round water crackers, some plain and some sprinkled with cracked pepper, as well as a few tart green apples. She was ready.

As she sliced the parmesan and laid it out next to the water crackers, she noticed the sun slanting lower through the bay window. In the distance, the sky was turning a deep shade of crimson just above the band of clouds at the horizon. Above, it transitioned to a deep indigo, where the lighthouse beam rhythmically passed. That didn't make it any less spectacular, however, and Maris let out a long breath. Even now she was thankful for having given up her corporate troubleshooting job. It'd taken no time to get used to the speed of things in Pixie Point Bay.

When Maris heard footsteps on the stairs, she turned away from the window, and a moment later, Kristofer Klaas entered the dining room. According to the B&B's records, he'd been a regular guest over the years, preferring Pixie Point Bay to the hotel in Cheeseman Village, even for longer stays. Although his bristly handlebar mustache was magnificent, it was his twinkling brown eyes that gave him a sense of youth that belied his probably middle aged years.

"Kristofer," she said, with a smile. She began to slice the green apples. "How nice to see you. I hope you've settled in well."

"Better than well, Ms. Seaver," Kristofer replied, taking a plate and beginning to serve himself cheese. "I wanted to thank you for keeping me so well fed. It makes things so much more pleasant when the evening wine and cheese can almost be a dinner." He poured some port for himself before turning back to her.

"I'm with you there," Maris said. "Maybe a little too with you," she added, taking a self-conscious glance down at her muffin top.

Looking back up at him, she said, "And please call me Maris. What is it that you do for a living, Kristofer?"

"I'm a glazier," he replied, taking a bite out of an apple slice.

"A glazier?"

"Someone who fits glass," he said. "It's the family business, actually. My grandfather brought the craft with him when he immigrated from Estonia."

"Estonia," Maris said. "Goodness, the old country is far away." She finished with the blue cheese and arranged it artfully on the board. "And what brings a glazier to Pixie Point Bay?"

"Restoration work," Kristofer replied. "It's sort of my specialty. I travel all over the area, taking appointments." He glanced out the window toward the ocean. "I must say, I'm impressed by the amount of work that's been put into this place. I guess there's a reason they call it the most beautiful lighthouse in the Middle Kingdom."

It didn't hurt that it was also located in one of the most picturesque spots on the West Coast. The pristine bay was nearly circular and ringed by dramatic cliffs. The lighthouse occupied the rocky point that jutted out at its southern end.

"You're preaching to the choir on that one," Maris agreed, laughing. "Even if I do say so myself."

He raised a hand. "Just telling it like it is."

The sound of more footsteps came from the stairs, and the pair turned to see the Longacre family making their way into the dining room.

"Not too much," Jen was saying to one of the twin daughters as she made a beeline for the snacks. "Don't spoil your dinner. We're going out for seafood." She gave Maris a polite smile as she and Tim, her husband, made their way to the refreshments. "Sorry about that," she said, nodding at her daughters, who were already loading up their plates. "They're just excited to be on vacation."

"No need to apologize," Maris replied, and made the introductions.

"Where are you folks coming from?" Kristofer asked.

"Colorado," answered Tim. "Boulder. We're here for the next week." He looked at Maris. "Thank you again for letting us take two of the rooms. It's a real treat for the girls."

"My pleasure," Maris said. "We're only at half capacity. Besides, I'm still settling in too."

They continued to make small talk as Jen went to get some juice for the twins. Tim poured wine for the adults, and Maris decided to sample the Prosecco. But all of them watched as the sun finally sank into the ocean, creating a rich, red reflection in the water that looked more like a mystical trail than a sunset. Maris finally felt the strangeness of the day retreating and her shoulders relaxed.

"Mojo," Kristofer said.

Maris looked down to see him squeezing past the glazier to get a better look at everyone. But as Kristofer stooped down and ran his fingers gently through the fluffy fur, the cat paused and purred. When he gazed up at the man, he gave his signature meow.

The twin girls descended on him when they heard the sound, squealing about how cute he was. Mojo, of course, waited patiently while they fawned over him.

"He's the perfect host," Jen said, smiling down at the trio.

Tim set down his empty glass, caught

Jen's eye, and tapped on his watch. She nodded and finished her port.

"Here we go, girls," their father said. "Dinner time."

Although there was a small protest, and a few last, long pets for Mojo, the Longacres headed out.

Kristofer loaded up a plate and poured another port before he turned to Maris with a smile under his spectacular mustache. "I've got an early appointment tomorrow so I think I'd better turn in." He lifted the glass to her. "Thank you again for another lovely evening."

She lifted her glass in return. "Sleep well."

Maris put away the uneaten refreshments, rinsed off the plates, and returned the port to its shelf. But when she opened the refrigerator to put the cheese and Prosecco away, she recalled the image of the fruit bowl back at the credit union. It had been brimming with grapes. Of that she was sure.

As she made her way back to her own room, with Mojo trotting behind, she puzzled over the entire day. From the moment that Millicent's face had soured to when she'd left the credit union, there were simply too many unanswered questions. But as she closed her door and Mojo jumped up on the bed, she knew the answers would have to wait until tomorrow.

6

In the morning, the enticing aroma of freshly brewed coffee wafted up the hallway as Maris approached the kitchen. Though she considered herself an early riser, Cookie was invariably in the kitchen first. Though their rooms were only a few feet apart, she never heard the chef get up or start cooking. But that didn't mean that Maris couldn't pitch in and help.

"Good morning," she said, with her usual morning cheer.

Cookie Calderon was standing in front of the stove, with heaping plates of food already next to her on the counter. Though she was a petite woman, and spry for her seventy years, Maris had no doubt she could still heft the iron skillets and dutch ovens that she favored.

"Good morning," she said, smiling at Maris over her shoulder. "How did you sleep?"

Cookie's straight, shoulder length hair was more salt than pepper these days, but her dark eyes still glinted with an inner light that never seemed to fade.

"Very well, actually," Maris replied, pouring herself a cup of coffee.

"So what's the news?" Cookie asked, still focused on the stove. "Trouble in town I take it."

Maris regarded her. "I didn't think you'd hear about Edwin so fast."

"Edwin?" Cookie asked, sliding a pancake onto one of the plates. "Edwin Martin at the credit union? I haven't heard anything. The Old Girl flashed her beam towards downtown while you were out yesterday." She nodded toward the back of the Victorian, where the lighthouse was located.

"Wait," Maris said, setting down her coffee. "The Old Girl, Claribel, pointed her beam at the town?"

Cookie glanced at her. "Didn't I mention she could do that?"

"I'm pretty sure not," Maris said, as

Cookie poured more batter. "She points her beam?"

"She has a knack for finding trouble," Cookie said and gestured with her spatula. "When she points at something you can be sure there's bad business afoot."

"Interesting," Maris said, drawing the word out.

"Your aunt and I used to wonder if that wasn't how the Old Girl compiled the best record of sea rescues in North America."

"No doubt magic helps," Maris said.

Cookie winked at her. "No doubt."

Maris and her aunt had shared not only the gift of precognition, but also the ability to remotely view something with the help of Claribel's fresnel lens. Cookie was a skilled maker of potions, and now it seemed the Old Girl had her own talent, aside from being a magical entity, of course.

Maris eyed the chef, wondering what else she might know.

"So what happened to Edwin Martin?" Cookie asked, and expertly flipped the pancake.

"He died," Maris said.

Cookie's eyes widened and her mouth dropped open. "You're kidding. Of what?"

"Well, that's the problem," Maris said. "No one's quite sure, and I was even there." She watched as Cookie cracked some eggs into a bowl. "Shall I make more pancakes while you mix the eggs?" Though Maris couldn't be sure, she thought Cookie hesitated.

"If you like," the older woman said.

Maris took a quick sip of her coffee and put some butter in the skillet. She recounted the entire afternoon at the credit union, trying to summarize the events without skipping the relevant details. Cookie listened as she started scrambling the eggs.

When Maris finished, the chef said, "Of course, one thinks of heart attack, but then again..." Cookie eyed her. "We would."

Not only had Maris's aunt died of one, but her mother as well. Maris had only been in high school. It was likely the reason that she'd never known she was a witch—her mother had thought she had time to tell her. Now it was Maris's turn to struggle with her weight and cholesterol, not to mention her Type A+ personality.

Maris shook her head as she poured some batter in the pan. "I don't think it was a heart attack. He was coughing, not having chest pain." She watched Cookie smoothly move the scrambled eggs around the pan, never letting them get too hard.

"Tomatoes and capers?" Maris asked.

"Yes," Cookie said, smiling. "They'll go quite nicely with the bagels and lox. We've got some very fresh cream cheese from Cheeseman Village too."

As Maris rinsed the tomatoes and put them on the cutting board, she saw a thin wisp of smoke out of the corner of her eye. "The pancake," she gasped. She snatched up the spatula but managed to tip over her coffee cup with it. It crashed to the floor. "Oops!"

Cookie calmly reached over and turned off the burner for the pancake. Even as she continued to stir the eggs, she took the paper towels from the holder and handed them to Maris.

"Thanks," Maris breathed. "*Sorry.*"

As she bent down and cleaned up the broken cup and spilled coffee, Cookie said something indistinguishable. Something about getting a life? "I'm sorry, Cookie," Maris said, still sopping up the liquid. "What was that?"

"I said I was looking for a knife," the chef said, not making eye contact.

By the time that Maris had the floor cleaned, the tomatoes were sliced, the eggs and pancakes were in their warming trays, and Cookie was plating the lox.

"Would you mind taking the warming trays to the dining room?" Cookie asked sweetly.

Maris blinked. Had it taken her that long to clean up the coffee? The older woman looked over at her. "Maris?"

"No," Maris blurted out. "I mean, yes." She paused and took a breath. "I mean I'd be glad to."

Though she had the distinct impression that she was being kept busy and out of the kitchen, she quickly went to the trays.

"It's not a race," Cookie said, as Maris picked up the first one. "It's an art."

Although Maris forced herself to move more slowly, it was only for Cookie's sake. Of course it was a race. Everything was a race. The only way that true hospitality came off as elegant and unhurried was when the staff moved at lightning speed behind the scenes. She'd based her whole career on it.

But as she fetched the next tray, she had to think about her career—the one that had burned her out. It'd been successful from the point of view of her employers, but what about her? As she set down the tray over the lit burner, she paused for just a moment to line the two trays up. She moved the butter as well. Cookie brought in the platter of bagels and lox. For a moment, the two of them simply admired the spread.

Maybe Cookie was right. Maybe it was an art.

As the diminutive chef headed back to the kitchen, she gave Maris a wink.

Maris had to grin, but as she glanced up at the dining room window, she nearly shrieked. In the dim light of the early morning fog, she didn't immediately recognize the hulking, bearded man standing outside and staring in at her.

She put a hand over her chest. *"Bear,"* she said, feeling her heart thump.

In response, he awkwardly lifted his giant hand and gave her the daintiest wave.

She exhaled and motioned the handyman toward the side porch. As she headed that way, she popped her head in the kitchen. "Bear is here," she told Cookie.

The older woman smiled. "I'll bring a tray."

William "Bear" Orsino was a mountain of a man, but as gentle as he was outsized. The upkeep on the Victorian buildings was almost constant, and the young man had become a fixture around the place. He was also one of the few magic folk about whom Maris knew any details.

When she met him on the porch, he ducked his head. "I didn't mean to scare you."

"Oh goodness," Maris said, smiling, "of course not. I'd never think that, even if I, you know, act like that."

She knew from Cookie that Bear was a shifter. Since he wanted to be home before nightfall, he liked to start his days early. He was dressed in his usual white t-shirt and bib overalls.

"Please," Maris said, indicating the patio's table and chair. "Have a seat."

His kind brown eyes looked to the back of the house. "Well, there's lots of work to do today. The back shutters need painting."

Cookie appeared with the breakfast tray and set it on the table. "Good morning, Bear."

Though he never took his eyes from the food, he said, "Good morning, Cookie." Maris noticed that the chef had used two plates, and heaped both full.

As though she heard his unasked question, the older woman said, "This is for you. I hope you enjoy it." With that, she retreated into the house.

His face lit up but he still hung back. Maris took out the chair for him. "Please, Bear. Sit and enjoy before it gets cold." Then it occurred to her that he might be shy because she was watching. "I'm going to...head to the lighthouse."

"Thank you," he said, sitting down and eagerly digging in.

"You're quite welcome," she said, and turned toward the tower.

Though it'd really just been an excuse to leave Bear in peace, Maris didn't know why she'd chosen the direction of the lighthouse until she was nearly there. If anyone could shed some light on the strange death of Edwin Martin, it would be the Old Girl. Just before she reached the doorway, a gusty breeze kicked up, swirling the fog and opening the tower's door.

7

———

The Pixie Point Bay lighthouse was a sturdy building whose white exterior and red trim matched the bed and breakfast perfectly. Nestled up against a craggy section of shoreline, it had originally been built in the late nineteenth century, with the lighthouse keeper's house being built the following year. Eventually the two buildings were connected together, although Maris always preferred to make the walk from one to the other outside in the fresh air.

Inside, as she flipped on the light switch, she said, "Good morning, Claribel."

Though there was no response, the door gently blew closed behind her.

Despite the fact that there were no furnishings, the interior had a timeless feel. The heavy metal staircase spiraled upward, its elegant curves accentuated by the decorative, vertical balusters. As she began the climb, Maris tried to imagine the craftsmen who had created it and wondered if they'd be pleased to know it was still in use.

By the time she had climbed to the second story, she was breathing hard but kept trudging upward. She gazed out the window on that level, grateful yet again that the builders had taken the trouble to install them. Finally at the top, she climbed the last step out onto the metal landing.

"Phew!" she exhaled as she paused for a moment taking in the view—and catching her breath.

Though the bay was still enshrouded in white mist, she could see the rocks below. The small waves rhythmically broke against them, their soothing sound easily audible in the early morning stillness. In the other direction Bear still sat on the porch enjoying his breakfast. It occurred to Maris that this view had likely changed very little in the last one hundred years. Although the original oil lamp that provided light for the lens had been replaced by LEDs, few other upgrades had been made. In fact, should those fail, she knew that Aunt Glenda had kept the lamp in storage.

The fresnel lens itself was more like a glass sculpture than something that anyone would recognize from a pair of glasses. Shaped almost like a giant egg, dozens of individual pieces of glass, some grooved with concentric circles, were tightly fitted together on a gleaming steel frame. It rose from its waist high pedestal up to nearly the top of the circular glass house where she stood. Its thousands of reflective surfaces bounced light in every direction, and it glowed as though it had a life of its own.

"How are you today, Old Girl?" Maris asked, careful not to look into the beam.

The lighthouse made no reply, but a sense of calm washed over her and a tingling warmth radiated from the lens. She closed her eyes for a moment before reopening them and gazed down into the faceted base of Claribel's lens. Sunlight danced within it like a prism, throwing out flecks of rainbow light that were entrancing. But suddenly an image began to form among the sparkles.

It was like looking through a telescope at

the Towne Plaza. The buildings passed by, one by one, and Maris expected that the credit union would soon come into view. But the viewing stopped at the medical clinic, its distinctly narrow front and yellow color unmistakable.

Maris's eyes narrowed. Why the medical clinic?

But as quickly as the image had popped into view, it vanished. Though she waited for another few moments, it seemed the remote viewing was over.

"Thank you," she said, and gave the pedestal an affectionate pat before beginning her descent.

Back outside on the ground level, the porch was empty so Bear must have finished his breakfast. But as Maris was approaching the porch door, he came down the side of the house from the gravel driveway.

"Maris?" he said, and held out a small jar to her. "This is for you and Cookie."

"Oh," she said, taking it from him. Inside the glass was the most deeply amber honey she'd ever seen. "What beautiful honey."

He ducked his head, looked at the ground, and folded his hands in front of his burgeoning middle. "I keep bees in my spare time."

"Do you?" she said. "Well thank you. I'm sure it'll be wonderful."

"You're welcome," he said, though he didn't look up. Without another word, he headed back down the steps and toward the rear of the house.

Back inside, Maris saw that Kristofer was sitting at the dining room table. True to his word, he was getting an early start on his day.

"Good morning," she said to him, pausing on her way back to the kitchen.

"It's a great morning," he said, spreading cream cheese on a bagel. "Would you tell Cookie that these are the fluffiest scrambled eggs that I have ever had? Marvelous. Who knew something so simple could be so good?"

Maris grinned back at him. "I'd be happy to pass that along. Do you have everything you need?"

He had just taken a bite of the bagel, tomato, cream cheese, and lox sandwich that he'd made. He rolled his eyes, shook his head, and gave her an emphatic okay sign.

In the kitchen, Cookie was rinsing more

tomatoes as Maris passed behind her. "Your scrambled eggs have conquered another happy stomach in the dining room. Kristofer Klaas sends his compliments." She placed the honey on the counter. "And Bear has given us some of his home grown honey."

Cookie dried her hands on her apron and picked up the jar. "Now this makes my day. I don't know what those bees eat, but you've never tasted anything as smooth and sweet."

"Shall I slice those?" Maris asked, indicating the tomatoes.

"Actually," Cookie said, picking up an empty plastic bin. "We're out of dishwasher soap pods. Would you be a dear and get some in town?"

There was that feeling again, as though what Cookie really needed was to simply get on with her work. Maris had never really learned to cook. Ironically, her hospitality career had precluded it. But pitching in to help was part of the life.

Then again, if you weren't a help?

"I'd be glad to get some in town," Maris replied, smiling.

Cookie took off her apron. "After we've had something to eat," she said.

This was a tradition at the Pixie Point Bay Lighthouse B&B that Maris had warmed to immediately. Rather than hide in the kitchen to eat, Cookie liked to share the morning meal with the guests.

Maris inclined her head and motioned for Cookie to precede her. "After we've had something to eat," she agreed.

8

Although Maris parked in front of the Main Street Market, she headed instead to the Pixie Point Bay Medical Clinic. Though she had no idea if Dr. Rossi would have any new information on Edwin Martin's death, Claribel hadn't shown her the clinic for no reason.

Seemingly squeezed in as an afterthought, the four-story building was as narrow as any she'd seen, even in the backstreets of ancient European towns. It was painted a bright and cheery yellow, and its elegant front French doors were welcoming. As Maris entered, however, it was like walking into a different world. The quaint exterior belied a sleek, modern and ultra clean interior.

A blonde, middle-aged woman wearing blue scrubs sat behind the reception counter. Embroidered near the V of her neckline was "Jill Maxwell, NP". It seemed that the clinic's nurse practitioner doubled as the receptionist.

She looked up from her computer screen and smiled pleasantly. "Good morning. How can I help you?"

"I was wondering if it would be possible to see Dr. Rossi today."

"Certainly," she said, using the computer mouse to click something on the screen. "He's with a patient right now but he should be available shortly. Do you have an appointment, Ms. ...?"

"Seaver," Maris replied. "Maris Seaver."

Jill typed in her name. "And what's the reason for your visit today, Ms. Seaver?"

Maris fumbled for a moment before saying, "My cholesterol." Unfortunately, it wasn't a lie.

The nurse typed some notes. "I'll let him know you're here for a walk-in. Please have a seat. He shouldn't be long."

"Thank you," Maris replied and headed to one of the modern white sofas.

As she sat down, she idly moved the magazines on the coffee table around. She found the latest issues of *Bassmaster, Saltwater Sportsman, and Fly Fisherman*, but Maris was neither the sporting type nor a fisherman. She was on the verge of leaving them be when she spotted the corner of the winter edition of *Lighthouse Digest*. She pulled it out of the stack to see a photo of a snow-dusted bridge leading to a charming lighthouse. She had just opened the front cover when the door to the back room opened and Dr. Rossi stepped out, accompanied by a mother and daughter, the latter of whom was sporting a bandaged knee.

"Thank you, Dr. Rossi," the mother was saying, giving him a warm smile.

"It's no trouble, really," the doctor assured her, returning the smile in kind. "Just keep it covered and clean and she'll be healed in no time. Call me if you have any questions."

He waved at them as they left the office, and then turned his attention to the next patient. But the moment he saw who it was, his face fell for a fraction of a second. Then his professional smile was back in place, and he beckoned to her.

"Ms. Seaver, this way, please."

She stood and followed him down the hallway into a small examination room. He gestured to the exam table with its covering of thin paper. She took a seat, as he closed the door.

He sat on a rolling stool on the other side of the room. "Well, what seems to be the problem, Ms. Seaver?"

"It's not a medical problem, actually," Maris replied, crossing her legs. "I just wanted to ask you a couple of questions about what happened yesterday at the credit union, if that's all right with you."

"Since you were there before me," the doctor said, "I doubt there's anything that I can add. But since I don't have a patient waiting, perhaps I can ease your mind about something."

"Thank you, Doctor." Maris cleared her throat, wondering briefly where to start. "Ashley was the one who called you yesterday?"

"Yes," he said, taking the stethoscope from his neck and putting it in his coat pocket. "She said she thought he may have choked on something. As you know, he was dead by the time I arrived."

"Right," Maris said. "I'm curious about how he seemed the last time you saw him. Was he in good health?"

"I'm afraid Patient-Physician privilege doesn't end with death," Rossi replied. "But I also understand the need to come to grips with a tragedy." He paused for a moment, as though weighing his words. "Frankly, I can't remember the last time I saw him before yesterday. You might say that he wasn't one for regular checkups."

"Regular checkups?" Maris said, cocking her head. "But you'd have seen him in the credit union. It's the only bank in Pixie Point Bay."

"I don't do my banking there," Rossi replied. "I bank in Cheeseman Village. Better interest rates. Besides, it's all online nowadays, anyway."

"True enough," Maris said. She considered for a moment. Patient-Physician privilege extending beyond death hadn't occurred to her. The only real questions she'd had for the doctor were medical in nature. "I guess that's really it, then. Thanks for your time, Doctor. I appreciate it."

"You're welcome, Ms. Seaver," Dr. Rossi replied, standing. He opened the door. "This way out."

It was just before she exited that one final question occurred to her. "Back at the credit union," she said, turning around, "you asked if Edwin had gone whale watching recently. Why?"

Dr. Rossi's brow furrowed. "Whale watching?" Maris nodded in the affirmative, and he rubbed the back of his neck. "I honestly can't remember asking that."

"You did, though," Maris told him.

The doctor shrugged. "I guess I was just making conversation."

At that moment, Nurse Maxwell appeared in the doorway. "Sorry to interrupt, Doctor. Your next appointment is here."

"Thank you, Jill," Rossi said before turning to Maris. "Sorry to cut this short, Ms. Seaver, but duty calls."

"Of course, Doctor," Maris said. "I'll see myself out. Thanks again."

～

JUST AS MARIS had been about to cross the Towne Plaza, her phone rang. She dug it out of her purse and frowned at the name that appeared on the screen: Geneva Tharald.

Though Maris had given her notice to Luguan Imperial Resorts weeks ago, apparently no didn't mean no. Ironically, when she'd been working for them, she and her boss had gotten on well—if only via telephone. Now Genie always seemed on edge.

Maris put on her game face and smiled. Rule number one in the hospitality trade was to be hospitable. Rule number two was never to burn a bridge. "Hi Genie, where in the world are you?"

This had been their standard greeting for years, except that Genie had generally been at the corporations headquarters in Miami and Maris had moved from city to city.

"Glitchy Heathrow," Genie answered, her voice tired. "It's a bit of an unplanned layover due to 'technical circumstances beyond their control'. How are you, Maris? Still in Pixie Point Bay?"

"I'm very well, thanks. And yes, still at the B&B."

There was a bit of a pause before Genie

said, "I was supposed to be in your neck of the woods tomorrow, the Napa property, but it looks like that's not going to happen."

Maris perked up. Although they'd only met in person a handful of times, they'd always enjoyed each other's company. "Are you thinking of stopping by?"

"Actually," Genie said, "I was wondering if you'd be tempted to meet me there. In fact, if you'd like to go early, the company can make it well worth your while."

Ah, Maris thought. *A different spin on the job offer.*

"I see," Maris said, letting her smile fade. "And if I were to actually go there, you probably wouldn't need to."

Although there was silence for a few moments, Genie finally said, "Probably."

Maris smirked. "Thanks for your honesty, Genie. I'm afraid the answer is still no."

"The higher-ups will give me a lot of leeway on this, Maris. It'd just be the Napa property. Knowing you, you'd have it sorted in a couple of weeks. What do you say?"

"I say," Maris said, smiling once more, "that I hope those IT guys in London get cracking so you can get to Napa."

Genie laughed a little. "All right. You can't blame a gal for trying." Maris heard a gate announcement in the background. "Great," Genie said. "This flight has been cancelled. I guess I better find another."

"Good luck," Maris said sincerely, "and happy landings."

"Thanks, Maris. You too."

9
____

Maris stepped up onto the sidewalk in front of the Main Street Market. Its two-story brick facade and stylish black awning hadn't changed for decades—which she counted as a good thing. Everything about the place said small-town general store, which is exactly what it was.

Maris entered through the antique wood door with its oval of finely etched glass, and stepped into her childhood. To the right was the expansive wood counter with ceiling-high shelves behind it. To the left were the completely packed aisles. But as she walked past the different rows of canned goods, home and bathroom supplies, and frozen dinners, she realized that she wasn't nearly familiar enough with the layout of the store to be able to navigate without help.

"Maris Seaver," said a familiar voice from behind her, "is that you?"

She turned to find the owner of the market, Howard Scry, at the end of the aisle and she couldn't help but smile. It was like looking at an encyclopedia page. The man's resemblance to Einstein was nothing short of remarkable. It helped that his crazy mop of hair was almost completely white, but Maris had always thought it was the matching bushy mustache that was the clincher.

"Yep," she answered. "Just me, Mr. Scry."

He rolled his large dark eyes in an exaggerated way. "How many times do I have to tell you to call me Howard? You're not that gangly, freckled teenager anymore."

"You can say that again," she said, laughing a little. "Old habits die hard...Howard."

"Indeed they do," he said. He beckoned her toward the front of the store. "Come on."

She followed him to the long wood counter. Next to the giant metal cash register was a row of large glass jars, each of which held sticks of candy in every color of the rainbow, and then some. A little thrill welled up in her. It was like being that teenager all over again.

"Root beer," he said as he took a tissue from the box on the counter and lifted the lid on the container that held the sticks of brown spiraled with beige.

Maris had to grin. He never forgot.

"A barber pole for the little lady," he said, handing it to her.

"Howard," she said, accepting it along with the tissue, "you are as sweet as your candy."

A little color rose to his cheeks, and Maris popped the end of the stick into her mouth. She could do with a little pick-me-up. Dieting could wait until tomorrow.

"How's business?" she asked, around the candy.

"The usual," he replied, replacing the glass lid. "Although everyone's abuzz about the unpleasantness yesterday."

"That was good of you to let his son know. Bryan said the doctor had called you."

Howard shrugged a little. "I never knew his father very well, so I can't say I'm too shaken up one way or the other. But his son has been fantastic here. A real hard worker." He paused and his considerable forehead furrowed. "Say, would you mind helping me out for a minute? I'd like your opinion on something, if you're not in too much of a hurry."

"I'm not," Maris said. "I just came for dish soap."

Howard jerked his thumb at the cash register. "It's about Bertha." Maris gazed at the enormous antique cash register. With metal gleaming, and glass shining, it seemed in perfect condition. Howard put his hands on his hips, appraising it for a moment. Then he turned back to her and said, "I'm thinking of upgrading her. Something a bit more modern. What do you think?"

"Bertha?" asked Maris. "What for?"

"Bryan says she's getting a little outdated," said the market owner. "He says a new one would be faster, more secure. And did you know that people can use their phones to pay these days? We live in strange times, I'll tell you." He shook his head. "Still, I'm not sold on it yet. I'm used to Bertha. I don't know if I'm ready to make that kind of a switch."

"Well, I can't really say what's secure and

what isn't, but I do know one thing." She waggled the barber pole at him. "You've got some of the most loyal shoppers in Pixie Point Bay. No matter what you decide, I'm sure they'll stick with you."

Howard grinned, perking up his bushy mustache. "Thank you." He glanced at the cash register again. "Well, it's something to think about at any rate. That Bryan is a smart kid. I bet it's all the seafood he eats. They say it raises your IQ, did you know that?"

"I didn't," Maris said, enjoying her candy. "Speaking of Bryan, have you talked to him today. How's he doing?"

"Well actually, he's here at work," Howard said. Seeing her reaction, he hastily added, "I didn't tell him he had to come in, mind you. I just couldn't force him to stay at home. He wanted something to keep him busy, so I fig-ured there was no harm in letting him come in for a few hours today. People handle stress differently."

"Of course, of course," Maris agreed. "Some people eat, and others can't." She glanced around. "Where is he? We met briefly and I'd like to say hi."

"Should be in the seafood section in the

back," replied Howard. "I'm sure he'd appreciate that." He paused for a moment. "You said dish soap, right? Let me see if I can find some for you."

He went to the door in back of the counter and disappeared behind it. In short order, Maris could hear the sound of bumping, then Howard's indistinct voice, then the sound of something scraping, and a crash. She smiled as she turned away. Some things were never going to change.

She found Bryan in the enormous seafood section putting fresh halibut fillets into the refrigerated case.

"Hey, Bryan," she said, wrapping up the rest of the candy stick in the tissue and tucking it in her purse.

He turned to look at her. "Oh, hey," he said, setting the bin of fish aside. "You're... Maris, right?"

"That's right," she replied. "Maris Seaver. Good memory."

There were bags under his eyes and he gave her a weak smile. "Thanks."

"Listen, Bryan," Maris said, "I just wanted to tell you again how sorry I am about your father. I have some idea of what you must be going through."

Bryan let out a long sigh, running a hand through his messy brown hair. "Thank you," he said. "I appreciate it. I'm sorry, too, that you were there when it happened."

"I'm fine," she said. "I just wanted to make sure you were okay."

Bryan shook his head. "I always told him he ate too fast, you know. I said if he didn't slow down something like this might happen." He sighed again. "I guess some people just don't listen."

He reached into the bin of fish and retrieved the last couple packages of halibut. Maris watched as he loaded them into the refrigerated case. Although the young man looked tired, he didn't seem particularly distraught. But looks could be deceiving. It could very well be that his father's death had not even sunk in yet.

People dealt with trauma in different ways. Some cried, tore their hair out, or slept for days, while others sometimes just shut down, all emotion seemingly gone as a defense mechanism. She wondered if Bryan was one of those latter types. Or maybe he just wanted to stay busy, which would be her choice too.

"How long have you been in Pixie Point Bay?" she asked.

"Not long," Bryan replied, finishing with the fish and moving to the end cap of the nearest aisle. "I was off at school for the past four years. I needed to get away, you know?" He opened a cardboard box of pickles. "I've only been back for a few months."

"Like me," Maris said, smiling. "What did you study in school?"

"History," Bryan said. "The job prospects aren't great for someone with that kind of degree. I'm looking, though." He picked up a big jar of pickles. "Maybe something at one of the nearby schools will open up. It's not like there's a museum around here for me to try."

Maris glanced around them. "At least you've got the supermarket until something else comes through." There was a pause. "Do you like working here?"

Bryan shrugged. "A bit. It's a job. I'll take what I can get. It could be worse, I guess." He glanced toward the front of the store, where they could still hear the faint sounds of Howard rooting through the storeroom.

"Howard's nice," he added. "A little weird, but nice."

Maris had to grin. "Most definitely nice." She paused for a moment. "When the funeral arrangements are set, I'll find out the details from Howard. You don't need to let me know personally."

Bryan blinked, his eyes wide, and for a moment Maris wondered if she'd said the wrong thing.

"I...I actually hadn't thought about that," he said, casting his eyes down to the floor. "I guess I do need to make arrangements, don't I?" He took a shaky breath. "I don't even know how, to be honest. I'm just moving into a new apartment. Where am I even supposed to start?"

"Well, you're the next of kin, right?" Maris asked. When Bryan nodded, she said, "I'm sure the Sheriff will be in touch with you soon. He can–"

"There you are," came a voice from behind them, causing them both to jump. Maris turned to see Dr. Rossi hurrying down the aisle toward them, still dressed in his white coat. "Maris, Bryan," he said, coming to a stop. "I'm glad I caught you both."

Maris cocked her head back. "You were looking for us?"

"Well, Bryan, specifically," he said. "But if you're here, Maris, all the better." He turned to the young man. "I was just wrapping up my last patient when I remembered something. I can't overstate how important this is. It has to do with your father."

A sudden crashing sound made Maris jump back. "What was..."

Shattered chunks of glass, whole pickles, and their brine covered the ground around Bryan's work boots. A little had splashed on Maris's skirt, but the young man's apron had been doused. Dr. Rossi had been in the line of fire as well, and a green stain was already forming at the hem of his white coat.

Bryan looked from him to Maris and back again, eyes wide, his mouth opening and closing for a moment. "I'm so sorry," he exclaimed. "I'm so sorry!" he said again. "I don't know what happened. Jeez, look at this..."

He nearly dove at the littered floor, getting down on hands and knees as he tried to stem the tide of the green liquid. As he cupped his hands, he made giant sweeping motions, trying to keep it from flowing under the shelves.

"Bryan," Maris said, reaching out a hand, "I don't think that's a good idea. I mean, you don't have to…"

But he wasn't listening, already scooping up pickles and pieces of the jar and dropping them into his apron, looking frantically around for something—maybe a bucket or towels.

"What's wrong with me?" he asked, shaking his head as he reached for a particularly jagged piece of broken glass.

A moment later he yanked his hand back, the broken pieces and gathered pickles falling back to the floor. He cradled his hand, examining it, and Maris could already see blood dripping onto the floor to join the pickle juice.

"Jeez," he muttered, hissing as vinegar worked its way into the cut.

"Let me see that," the doctor said, taking Bryan's hand gently and holding it up to the light. He frowned, and looked ready to say something when Howard came around the corner and into the aisle, a plastic bin of dish soap in his hand.

"What happened?" he asked.

"I'm so sorry, Mr. Scry," Bryan nearly shouted. "I dropped a pickle jar. I cut myself. I– Ouch," he exclaimed as the doctor moved his hand slightly.

"It's all right, Bryan," Howard said, his tone soothing. "Just take it easy. A jar of pickles isn't the end of the world. I'll get this cleaned up." He handed the dish soap to Maris.

"This is going to need cleaning and stitches," the doctor said. "We can do that at the clinic."

"You go with the good doctor," Howard told the young man, who had lost a bit of color. "He'll take care of you."

"Okay," Bryan muttered.

Howard gave him a gentle pat on the shoulder. "Good boy."

"It's not as bad as it looks," the doctor was saying as he led him away.

10

Dish soap in hand, Maris returned to her car. But rather than go home with it, she stowed it in the back seat and took out the canvas bag. In it was her crochet project, two balls of yarn, and her various crochet hooks.

As she strolled to the crochet club, she glanced over at the medical clinic. Even if Bryan had wanted to be busy today, he probably shouldn't have gone to work. Although she'd likely have done the same, the poor boy had obviously not been in shape for it. She made a mental note to check on him occasionally over the next few days.

As she ascended the steps to the By Hook or Crook Crochet Club, she saw movement through the sheer curtains behind the front door's windows. Her finger was poised above the doorbell when the front door flew open, revealing the home's owner and the president of the club.

"How nice to see you again, Maris," Millicent said, her eyes smiling. She stood aside and held the door open. "Why don't you come in?"

"Thank you very much," Maris replied, "and thank you for your invitation."

"Glad you've finally decided to join us," Millicent said as she closed the door behind them and beckoned for Maris to follow her down the hall.

The front room was impeccably decorated, with embroidered armchairs set up in a circle in front of the fireplace, where a cheery fire burned. In each of these sat a woman of a similar age to Millicent, working on crochet projects in every color possible. At the sound of footsteps in the doorway, they raised their heads, giving the newcomer welcoming smiles.

"Ladies," Millicent said, putting an arm around Maris's shoulders, "we have a new club member. Please say hello to Maris Seaver. She runs the bed and breakfast at the lighthouse." The circle of women murmured hellos, smiling, as Millicent introduced them. "Maris, I'd like you to meet Zarina," she said, indicating a stout woman with a bandana tied around her head. "This is Helen," Millicent continued, pointing to a bespectacled woman, who gave Maris an eager smile. "Eunice," she said as she pointed to a bottle redhead with more wrinkles than Maris thought possible. "And this is Vera." She gestured towards a portly woman with short gray hair.

"Let me get you a chair," Eunice said, standing up and grabbing another armchair from the corner of the room. As she dragged it over, the other ladies scooted their chairs to make room. Maris took the chair from her and carried it the rest of the distance.

"Thanks for having me," she said, as she took a seat. She fidgeted with her project and supplies for a moment, acutely aware of how scrambled her little scarf looked.

"It's our absolute pleasure," Millicent said, giving her a wide grin as she took her seat near the fire. "In fact," she added, exchanging an unreadable look with the other women, "we were kind of hoping you would drop by, weren't we, girls?"

The other ladies nodded, murmuring their agreement. "We heard you were at the credit union yesterday," Vera said, glancing briefly at Millicent. "Terrible. Just terrible." She looked over her glasses at Maris's scarf and her eyebrows flew up.

Zarina shook her head, adding, "What a horrible way to spend your afternoon. I hope you're feeling well."

"I'm doing fine," Maris replied, beginning to crochet. "But I don't might telling you, it was a bit rattling."

"Would you mind telling us what happened?" asked Helen, leaning forward in her chair a little. "Everyone in town is buzzing about it, but we still haven't gotten anything from the horse's mouth, so to speak."

"Of course," Maris said.

In truth, she'd been expecting exactly this conversation. If there was any new information to be had, surely it would have reached the ears of the crochet club by now. Maris would do her part by offering up her observations, and she would then expect something in return.

With the exception of the missing grapes, she explained everything that happened, starting with her trip to open an account and giving them as many details as she thought they'd want about the death itself. But she was careful not to embellish either, especially since this was her third telling, after Mac and Cookie.

As Maris told her story, she had their rapt and unflinching attention. The ladies nodded, shook their heads, and clicked their tongues almost as one.

"...and then Dr. Rossi showed up at the market," she said, trying to untangle a knot in her yarn. "Bryan dropped a pickle jar and cut his hand on one of the broken pieces."

Vera sucked in a sharp breath. "Ooh, is he okay?"

"He should be fine," Maris said, giving up on the knot and taking out her scissors. "The doctor was escorting him to the clinic when I left. He said he would need stitches, but that it wasn't serious."

"Well, thank heaven for that," Millicent said, deftly stitching a chain of three loops in a split second. Her project was also a scarf but it was a kaleidoscope of colors, and astonishingly bright.

Helen was crocheting a doily with a

needle so small that Maris could barely see the hook. Eunice was creating a floppy white hat with a delicate pattern of gay flowers on the front.

Zarina looked up from her baby boot. "That poor boy has been through enough. Poor Dr. Rossi, too."

Maris kept her expression bland and her voice neutral. "What do you mean, 'poor Dr. Rossi'?"

Zarina glanced in Millicent's direction, and the president of the club gave her a small nod. It was the moment that Maris had hoped for.

"The credit union foreclosed on his home," Zarina said, dropping the volume of her voice a notch. "His wife divorced him after that. Probably just too much strain on their marriage. She left Pixie Point Bay and took their two daughters with her."

"Terrible," Vera remarked, shaking her head. "Just terrible." The others murmured their agreement.

"Believe it or not," Zarina continued, "Edwin Martin was the one who took possession of Dr. Rossi's house. He lives in it, or rather, lived in it. Well, Bryan lives in it, at any rate. I guess he'll be inheriting everything Edwin owned."

"Did he own a lot?" Maris asked, tying a new piece of yarn to the string she'd cut.

"Oh, yes," replied Zarina. "There's the house, a yacht, and four rentals. That Edwin Martin made his fortune on the bad luck of other people."

"The shameless, greedy man," Millicent said, looking as if she could spit.

The ladies nodded their agreement. "Pixie Point Bay is better off without him," Helen said, her expression grave. "Whoever killed him should get a medal, if you ask me." Millicent loudly cleared her throat, and Helen dropped her gaze to the floor.

Maris, however, had already noticed the gaff. "Nobody said it was a murder," she said quietly, looking around the circle of ladies.

In the sudden silence of the room, the ticking of the antique clock sounded like hammer blows. Vera sniffed, Zarina stared down at her project, and Millicent pursed her lips. The silence stretched on for another few seconds before Millicent said, "So what are you crocheting, Maris?"

11

———

*I*t's never as straightforward as they make it *look on TV*, Maris thought as she turned off the engine of her rental car. She fished the dish soap and canvas bag out of the back seat, and stepped out onto the manicured gravel in front of the B&B. The detectives on the shows always got the information in the exact order they needed it, with no contradictions and no dead ends. And yet here she was, with the help of a magical lighthouse no less, and nothing was adding up. There was no trail to follow, and she had even been there.

Maris let herself in the front door. Judging from the lack of cars in the parking slots, the guests were all out for the day.

"Cookie?" she called, pulling her purse off her shoulder.

"In here," came Cookie's voice from the living room. Maris followed the sound to where the chef was sitting in one of the high back chairs, an open book in her lap. "Did you get lost?" she joked, quirking an eyebrow at Maris as she sat down across from her.

"No," Maris replied, putting the plastic container of soap pods on the coffee table. "I did poke around a little, though. About Edwin Martin."

"Oh?" Cookie said, closing her book and removing her glasses. "And where did you do this poking around?"

"I started by talking to Dr. Rossi," Maris said as she settled into her chair. "He wasn't able to tell me much. Then, when I was at the supermarket getting the dish soap, I talked a little bit to Bryan Martin."

"How's he doing?" Cookie asked.

"Surprisingly well," Maris replied. "I think he might just be a bit numb to the whole thing." She shook her head and continued. "The doctor startled us and Bryan dropped a jar of pickles, then cut himself cleaning up the broken glass."

Cookie's brow furrowed. "Is he all right?"

"I think so," Maris said. "Rossi took him back to his clinic for stitches. Speaking of which," she added, pulling her mess of a crochet project out of her bag, "I stopped by the By Hook or Crook Crochet Club on my way back."

"Is that right?" asked Cookie, putting her book aside. "How's Millicent?"

"She seems very well," Maris told her. "She was working on a scarf that was just out of this world. The colors were simply unreal. It was like a kaleidoscope."

"Well, that makes sense," Cookie said. "I happen to know that she reads auras."

"Auras?" Maris's eyes widened. "As in spiritual energies?"

"Exactly," the chef said. "She crochets with colors that are out of this world because she sees colors that are out of this world. Have you ever thought about how she always seems to know exactly what's going on in town, and in everyone's personal lives?"

"Of course," Maris said. "I thought that was just because she was a busybody."

"Well actually, that doesn't hurt," Cookie conceded.

"Huh," Maris said, tilting her head. "It makes sense. I had a feeling she might be one of the magic folk, but I would never have guessed aura reader."

"If anyone has the pulse of the town," Cookie said, "it's Millicent and her bunch."

Maris couldn't agree more. "They told me Edwin took possession of the doctor's house."

"Oh yes, I heard about that," Cookie said.

"So it's true, then?"

"Oh indeed. The town was buzzing about it for a while after it happened. Nobody should have to lose their house and family all at once like that. And somehow Edwin always managed to come out on top—which of course makes you wonder about Bryan."

"What do you mean?"

"His father was one of the wealthiest men in Pixie Point Bay," Cookie replied. "Why would his son need to work a job at the supermarket?"

"That's a good point," Maris said, considering for a few moments. Was it perhaps part of Bryan's determination to be busy?

"Don't forget about Millicent," Cookie added. "She would have seen Edwin's aura.

Maybe she could shed some light on his situation."

"Definitely. Did I mention that Helen, one of the other women at the club, said whoever killed Edwin should get a medal?" She narrowed her eyes. "The crochet club knows more than they're saying."

"Of course they do," Cookie replied. "That's because they're not a crochet club. Not really." Seeing Maris's look of confusion, she added, "They're more like a cabal of busybodies. Practically a syndicate of spies, if you ask me. Those women see and hear everything, and it all ends up finding its way back to Millicent."

"Interesting," Maris said. "Sounds like it's worth doing some more digging."

A tiny, tinny, harmonica-like meow interrupted them, and drew Maris's attention to the hallway. Mojo stood there, his orange eyes fixed on her. He meowed again, turned back to the hallway, and then looked at her over his shoulder. With one final meow, he padded away.

"I think I'm being paged," Maris said, standing. Cookie got up as well and they both followed Mojo into the hallway, where he disappeared into the parlor.

In the elegant entertaining room, the ouija board sat in its usual place on the coffee table. What had once been a novelty for guests had become an object of greater interest for Maris since she'd discovered that Mojo liked to interact with it. Not only did he occasionally move the planchette, he sometimes spelled complete words.

This time, however, the fluffy cat ignored the ouija board, instead bouncing over to a box of tarot cards, which had overturned on the floor, the cards scattered everywhere. Cookie muttered something under her breath and moved to start picking them up, but Maris held a hand out.

"Hang on a second," she said, watching as Mojo took a seat by the pile. He waited patiently, as if to make sure he had their attention, and then, ever so gently, he touched one of the cards with his paw. After a second or two, he reached out and touched it again, his movements deliberate.

As Mojo watched in seeming fascination, Maris picked it up. Turning it over, and then right side up, she read its title. "The Moon."

Not surprisingly, it held an illustration of a crescent moon in the night sky. It hung low between two towers, illuminating a small body of water in the foreground. Out of this pool crawled a small crayfish, and beyond it in a grassy field were a dog and a wolf, their snouts turned upward as they howled.

"Any idea what this means?" she asked, handing the card to Cookie.

"Not a clue," she said, "but there should be a little booklet that comes with the deck."

Maris found it, still inside the box. "Let's see," she said. "According to this, I picked it up in the reversed position. In that case, the moon corresponds to repressed emotion, inner confusion, and the release of fear."

She gave Cookie a puzzled look, while the chef lifted her shoulders as she handed the card back to Maris. "I'm not feeling particularly repressed."

"And I don't think either of us has much fear," Maris said and looked down at Mojo, who seemed to be listening to them. "And you, Mojo, are you experiencing inner confusion?"

In answer, he simply gave his signature meow, and bounced out of the room.

Cookie stooped to pick up the cards. "Looks like Mojo found something else as well." She picked it up and handed it to Maris. It was a candy bar wrapper.

Grimacing and feeling heat rise in her cheeks, Maris took it from her. Mojo must have gone into her purse. She'd need to start making sure it was zipped closed. She crumpled the wrapper in the palm of her hand.

"Looks like there's more than one sleuth in the family," Cookie remarked drily, but was good enough not to mention Maris's diet.

"I'll put away the cards," Maris said, and quickly bent to the task.

12

With another successful evening of wine and cheese behind her, and the guests in their rooms or out to dinner, Maris rinsed the last few dishes before loading them in the dishwasher. Once that was done, she added the soap pod, set the machine running, and began the breakfast setup. Though she never managed to make it to the kitchen before Cookie in the morning, she tried to do her part. She ground just the right amount of coffee beans and put the grounds in a sealed container. She added water to the brewer and also the hot water dispenser. But there was no need to clean the stove, ovens, or microwave. Like any good craftsman, Cookie always left everything clean and organized for the next meal.

Maris was reaching out to the light switch to flick it off, when the sound of gentle tapping came from the back porch door. As she made her way through the hallway and front rooms, then back toward the porch's vestibule, she couldn't imagine who would be knocking at this hour. But when she saw through the glass who stood there, she was doubly puzzled.

"Slick," she said, opening the door for the aged fisherman. "Goodness. What are you doing here?" She paused when she realized how that must have sounded. "I mean, it's wonderful to see you." She held her arms out for a hug. "But what brings you out at this hour?"

Like clockwork, in the early morning and late afternoon, he and his commercial fishing boat passed the lighthouse on his way to and from the open ocean. Even at this moment, he was dressed for the job wearing his bright yellow slicker and matching hat.

He took the pipe out of his mouth to return her embrace, his long white beard draping behind her shoulder. "Maris

Seaver," he said, holding her gently. Maris closed her eyes and breathed in the warm scent of a sunlit ocean. After a few moments he pulled back, but he held her at the shoulders. "How much you remind me of your aunt."

Though he smiled, his soft voice carried a tinge of sadness, and Maris knew why. Though he and Glenda had both been in their eighties, they'd had a relationship. There was a familiar twinge in her chest.

"I miss her too," Maris said.

His deeply green eyes seemed a bit misty, but he just nodded once as he let her go. Then he peered past her into the B&B. "There's things that need to be discussed," he said. "Alone. Why don't you come down to the boat with me."

That sounds ominous, Maris thought, but said, "Of course," as she closed the door behind her.

Together they made their way down the stone steps carved into the rocks below the lighthouse, then out onto the narrow wood dock. Slick's sky blue boat with its red and white trim, *Seas the Day*, was roped to the pier's cleats. Above them, Claribel's beam easily penetrated the darkness and revolved in a slow, comforting circle.

"Here," he said, climbing aboard before extending a hand to her. "Come sit with me for a while."

"Thank you," Maris said, allowing him to help her up onto the boat.

Though tall and thin, Slick was incredibly strong, and Maris wondered if it was from his lifetime of fishing. He turned over a crate, brushed it off with his hand, and gestured for her to take a seat. Maris gratefully did so, not expecting to feel quite so unbalanced with just the small waves from the bay. Slick seemed to be having no problem at all.

Maris gazed around at the cluttered deck. "What's that cage for?" she asked.

He picked it up. "Crabs," he said, as though he was amused. "Did I ever tell you about the one that got away?" Maris shook her head. "It was as big as a suitcase."

She gave him a skeptical look. "Oh really. If it were that big, it wouldn't have fit in that cage."

"No, it wouldn't," Slick agreed. "I didn't catch it in a cage. I was line fishing for striped marlin that day. Reeled it in by accident."

Maris gave him an indulgent smile. "I see. And was it a world record of some sort? Biggest crab ever caught?"

Slick shook his head, a look of regret passing over his face. "Like I said, it got away."

He nodded to the railing on the far edge of the boat. "Grabbed the boat right there."

Maris obliged him with a glance to the railing, but then did a double take. Large, regular gouges scarred the edge and the side of it, the paint stripped in places. Though she might have only eaten crab a dozen times in her life, she could picture how the notches of an enormous claw could leave those marks. Her eyebrows rose.

"Just about had him aboard when he used his other claw to snip the line." He made a cutting motion with his fingers. "Never seen the like."

"No," she said, finally taking her eyes from the damage. "I don't imagine you have."

For a few moments there was silence, nothing but the sound of the water lapping against the boat.

"But I didn't bring you down here to tell

you stories about crabs," Slick said, setting aside the cage.

"No," Maris agreed. "I expect you didn't."

"I'll scupper the chit chat, then," Slick said. "I heard that Martin guy—the credit union manager—died yesterday. Is that right?"

"Yes, I was there."

"Right, that's what I heard," Slick said. "That's why I wanted to talk to you." He took the pipe from his pocket. "You have a nose for these things, Maris." He took out a plastic lighter. "I pass the man's yacht when I'm coming and going at the pier. It's moored not too far from where I dock." He lit the pipe and took a few deep puffs.

"And?" Maris asked, leaning forward.

"I'm getting to it," Slick replied, motioning her to slow down. "You and Glenda," he said, teasingly, but looked into her eyes. "I saw someone on the yacht."

"Who?" Maris asked, her pulse quickening.

"Dr. Rossi," he said, then took another puff.

Her eyes widened. "Are you sure it was him?"

"I wasn't at first," he admitted. "He wasn't wearing that white doctor's coat he usually wears. But my eyesight's pretty sharp. It was him, all right."

"What was he doing? Did you get a good look?"

"Oh yes," Slick said, nodding sagely. "He'd gotten himself into a bit of a fix."

"What do you mean?"

"Somehow he'd managed to get onto the yacht but it had drifted a little and dropped a foot or two with the tide change. By the time I showed up, he was jumping up and down on the deck trying to reach the pier's ladder."

Maris leaned back on her crate. "Good grief," she muttered. It sounded like something that could have happened to her.

"So I brought *Seas the Day* alongside the yacht," Slick continued, "and helped the doctor climb aboard and took him back to the pier. Must have been in some hurry. Rushed off without a word of thanks."

Maris pursed her lips. "No doubt he was preoccupied."

"Maybe," Slick said, noncommittally.

"But why are you telling me this?" Maris

asked. "Surely this is something to bring up with the sheriff."

"Eventually, sure," Slick conceded, peering out at the ocean. The full circle of the moon floated on its inky surface. "But I wanted to let you know first, give you a chance to run through it all with that brain of yours."

"Why?" she asked.

Slick leaned forward, fixing her with a piercing gaze. "Because," he said, his tone hushed and conspiratorial, "you're one of the magic folk. The sheriff is first-rate, but I don't think he really fathoms our little town. The doc isn't one of the magic folk either." He sat back. "You follow your heading, Maris. It'll lead you to the truth."

"You know," she mused, thinking back on that afternoon, "at the credit union, after Edwin died, Dr. Rossi made a comment about whale watching. I thought it was a little strange, and it's stuck with me. And now you're saying he was on Edwin's yacht after he died. Interesting."

"Interesting indeed," Slick agreed.

13

As usual the next morning, Maris woke up before her alarm. Though she couldn't remember dreaming about her conversation with Slick, she must have since it was immediately top of mind. The doctor had to be connected to Edwin Martin's death in some way other than the obvious—being the first medical person to see the body. But how he could be linked with the manager's demise wasn't clear, at least not with the information at hand. She had to keep digging, but she also knew she needed to let Mac know.

When she turned on the nightstand lamp, Mojo stirred at her feet. He raised his head to look at her but then let it flop back down on her ankle.

"Good morning to you too," she said quietly.

As she reached for her phone where it was plugged in next to the lamp, the bedroom suddenly vanished. For just a moment she wondered if the lamp had gone out, and then she could smell a barbecue. Though this had only happened once before, Maris recognized her precognition ability.

She was no longer in her bedroom at the lightkeeper's house. It was the crowded, wood-paneled interior of Delia's Smokehouse in Pixie Point Bay's plaza. Though she hadn't been there recently—in service of her diet—she'd know it anywhere. The smell of grilled fish continued to intensify, enough to make her mouth water. The din of conversation and clinking of silverware filled her ears.

But as quickly as it had begun, the vision of the future ended and instead she heard her cellphone ringing. The caller ID said it was Mac. She blinked a few times before answering.

"Mac" she said, sitting up. "Good morning."

"Good morning," he said. "I hope I'm not calling too early."

"Not at all. Early mornings are standard around here."

"Good," he said. "Let me get right to the point. I have some news about the Edwin Martin case."

"Information?" Maris asked.

"So to speak," he replied. "And I wanted you to hear it from me."

Maris frowned, and Mojo lifted his head to stare at her. Mac sounded so serious. "What is it?" she asked, almost not wanting to know.

"It's Dr. Rossi," he told her. "He was struck by a vehicle behind the clinic. Hit and run."

Maris's hand flew to her mouth. "Oh no, is he..."

"He was unconscious but alive when the paramedics took him."

She let out a breath. "Oh thank goodness." Mojo sat down next to her hip, and put a paw on her leg. She absently ran her fingers over the top of his head. "I can't imagine this is coincidence."

"I'm not saying the two things are connected," Mac said, "but I'd have to agree."

Finally she recalled what Slick had told her. "I have some information for you, too,"

Maris said, her mind racing. "Is there some place we can meet to talk in person?"

"Yes," Mac replied immediately. "I'm at the medical clinic right now. The EMTs just left. If you want, we can meet here."

"Okay, yes. Perfect. I'll be there ASAP." There was a pause, and she added, her tone softening, "Thanks, Mac. I appreciate your calling."

"You're welcome, Maris," he replied, and hung up.

Maris picked up Mojo before she swung her legs over the side of the bed. But when she put her foot down, it landed on something soft and squishy. She yanked her foot back up and peered at the floor. There, on the ornate Persian rug, was what looked like a velvet banana.

"What in the world?" she muttered. With Mojo tucked under her arm, she reached down and picked it up. To her surprise, it *was* a velvet banana. But as she held it up to the light, she saw some lettering stitched along its side: Catnip.

"Mojo," she said, reprovingly.

His toys were everywhere. But despite the

fact that she'd stumbled across a number of them, she never saw the same one twice.

"Where are you hiding all these?" she asked him.

But his only answer was a plaintive mewing, as he looked from the toy to her.

"Here you go," she said, putting them both on the floor. He immediately flopped down on top of it.

Maris went into the bathroom to run the shower, but paused to eye the scale on the floor. As usual, it was looking squatly malevolent. One of the few advantages of living in hotel rooms for your job was never having to be confronted with these things. But here it was again, glaring at her. Well, she was not going to be intimidated.

She stepped over to it, then on top of it, and watched the digital number appear.

"Up one pound?" she said, almost wailing.

She stepped off and used her foot to nudge it into the corner, as far as it could possibly go. Tomorrow she'd find a place for it in the closet.

14

Just as it had been yesterday, Maris noted that the lobby of the Pixie Point Bay Medical Clinic was empty except for Jill Maxwell. Yet somehow it felt different. Perhaps it was the fact that she knew the doctor was fighting for his life, or maybe it was the anxious look that the nurse practitioner gave her.

"I'm sorry," Jill said, "the clinic is closed for the day. There's been an accident. The doctor isn't available."

"I know," Maris said, closing the door behind her. "That's why I'm here. Sheriff McKenna asked me to meet him."

"Oh," Jill said, relaxing a little. "Well, that's a relief. The sooner this is sorted out, the sooner I can start to see patients who don't want to wait for Dr. Rossi."

"I totally understand," Maris told her.

Jill looked down the hallway that led to the exam room. "He's in the–" A door a few feet further down opened and Mac exited. "Well, here he is."

The sheriff strode down the hall directly to Maris. "I'm glad you could make it," he said. "Thanks for coming so quickly."

"Of course," she said. "Anything that I can do to help."

He turned to the nurse. "Jill, I'm going to bring Maris to the back for a minute, all right?" Jill nodded, and without another word the sheriff turned on his heel, motioning for Maris to follow him. "I think you're going to want to see this."

Her curiosity piqued, Maris followed him past the examination room and into a small maintenance room no bigger than a closet. Mounted on the desk was an old-fashioned video monitor, and next to it a stack of sleek, black electronic boxes. On the screen was a grainy, black and white image that could only have come from a security camera.

"We were going through the security footage earlier this morning," Mac said, leaning down toward the electronics, "and we found this." He pressed a play button on one of the boxes, and the image began to move. Maris peered over the sheriff's shoulder at the screen, having to squint to make out the grainy shapes. "This was taken from the alley around the back of the clinic," Mac said, leaning forward as the two of them watched the footage.

"That has to be Dr. Rossi," Maris said, pointing to the white-clad figure emerging from the left side of the frame. She understood what she was about to see and swallowed in a dry throat.

"Right," Mac said, and they stared at the pixelated figure as he made his way down the alley to where a car was parked. Nothing seemed out of the ordinary, which only made Maris more nervous. But one second later, there was a bright flash of light and the doctor was illuminated at waist level. It had to be the headlights of a car.

"Move," Maris urged him. "*Move.*"

The rest happened in quick succession: a car sped into the scene; Dr. Rossi waved his arms frantically; then he tried to dive out of the way; the car struck him and he flew out of the frame, along with the car.

Her hand flew to her chest, and it was all she could do not to shriek. *The poor doctor.*

In front of her, Mac hadn't seen her reaction. He paused the footage then reversed, zooming in so they could get a better look at the windshield. The figure behind the wheel was shrouded in darkness and wearing black gloves, his or her face unidentifiable.

"Any idea who that is?" Mac asked.

Squinting it at, Maris shook her head. "I'm afraid not. I can't see enough of the driver, and I don't recognize the car."

"Actually, we have a positive confirmation on the license plate. That's Edwin Martin's car."

Maris gave him an incredulous stare. "More than a little macabre," she said. A dead man's car had been used to try to kill another. "How is the doctor doing?"

"Stable," Mac replied, his brow furrowing. "They have him in a medically-induced coma in Cheeseman Village. Apparently he arrived with multiple fractures and internal bleeding. They're not sure if he's going to make it."

Maris had to wince. "I can't say I'm surprised after seeing that footage. But I'll keep a good thought for him."

"Your turn," Mac said, straightening up and crossing his arms. "You said you had some information of your own."

"I do," Maris replied, taking a step back from the monitor. "I talked to Slick Duff last night. He said he saw the doctor on Edwin Martin's boat yesterday."

"On his boat?" Mac said, stroking his chin for a moment. "That's very interesting."

"Why?" she asked.

"Because we went through Dr. Rossi's possessions," he said. "On his person were transdermal patches. You know, the kind you use to quit smoking...or to control seasickness."

The gears in Maris's head were already turning. "Do you think he was planning to be at sea by trying to steal the yacht? It sounds like he had a bone to pick with Edwin."

"I don't know," replied Mac, pushing the door open and leading her back to the lobby. "We're having the patches sent in for testing. I'll let you know once the lab results come in."

"Thank you, Mac," Maris said, feeling at last like the pieces were starting to come together. She would like to have chatted longer too, except that she could see out the window that Millicent Leclair was under the gazebo in the Towne Plaza.

"Listen," she said, "I've got to go. Thank you for the information, Mac. If I find out anything else, I'll let you know."

"Thanks, Maris," Mac replied. "I'd appreciate it."

15

As Maris approached the gazebo, Millicent gave an excellent imitation of being surprised. "Maris," she exclaimed, despite having watched her walk over. "What brings you into town again?"

"I was visiting the clinic," Maris replied, deciding not to add, *as you well know*. "The sheriff asked me to meet him."

"Oh he did, did he?" Millicent said, in that tone of voice that said she'd catalogued that fact away for later. "I have to say, I'm worried about that poor doctor. The ladies and I heard he was in some kind of a car crash?"

Maris considered for a moment before replying. In this negotiation, she had the upper hand.

"You might say I have some insight into what happened to the doctor," she began slowly. "I wouldn't call it especially perceptive, like maybe seeing, say, his spiritual energy. But I might have seen something else."

Millicent's eyes narrowed to slits. "I see," the older woman said through tight lips.

Maris smiled at her. "I know you do." Millicent inclined her head slowly, as if in acknowledgement. "I'll tell you what," Maris continued. "I can tell you what I know about the doctor, if you'll tell me why Helen said Edwin Martin was *murdered*."

"Oh, that's not a problem," Millicent said, seeming like her old self. "We'd been watching that one for months. Little revelations regarding his vile business practices kept coming to light, like the muck from an overturned stone. The longer we observed him, the more he showed his true nature. It was only a matter of time before we could prove something." She sniffed and drew herself up. "Of course, I knew it years ago. His aura screamed it."

Now the older woman sat back, primly placing her hands on her knees, and pointedly looked at Maris.

"It wasn't a car accident," she said, choosing her words carefully. By the time the day was done, this information would have reached the ears of all the other ladies in the crochet club, and who knows how much farther. "It was a hit-and-run." Millicent gasped. "At least, that's what it looked like on the security camera video." Maris paused for effect, looking left and right before leaning in. "But here's where it gets really strange." Millicent came forward on her seat. "Whoever it was who ran the doctor over, they did it with Edwin Martin's car."

Millicent opened her mouth as if to say something, but quickly closed it, blinking and then coughing as though she'd just swallowed a fly. Although Maris smiled inwardly, she couldn't blame her; even someone with the aura reader's gift wouldn't have been able to see that one coming.

As Maris crossed the rest of the Towne Plaza, still enjoying the moment with Millicent, her phone rang. She took it out of her purse, and was surprised at who was calling.

"Genie," Maris said, "where in the world are you?"

"Freaking Heathrow," Genie said, her voice a little raspy and deep.

Maris scowled as she continued her walk. "Still?"

"Yes, still," her former boss said. "I had to sleep at the gate because, get this, the company didn't want to pay for a hotel next to the airport."

If Maris could count the number of times that Luguan Imperial Resorts had pinched a penny at her expense, she'd count well into the hundreds.

"I'm sorry to hear that," Maris said, and she was—but not too sorry. This was part and parcel of the trade. Travel was never a slam dunk.

"Look, I'm getting a lot of pressure from Pam, but I don't have time for another hiring search and recruiters who can't deliver. She's willing to give you a bonus on the Napa property."

Pamela Watson was Genie's boss. Maris had only met her once, in Miami. She'd struck her as a slave to the ledger, someone who saw the bottom line with a lot more focus than the people it represented.

"Genie, I'm sorry," Maris said, arriving at her car. "But these calls are really just a waste of your time. I've got a new life now. The company is in the past. I hope you can see it from my point of view."

"Yeah, yeah," Genie said, sounding exhausted. "All right. I've got to go find some congealed pasta or a burned burger or something."

With a generous helping of saturated fat on the side, Maris thought grimly.

"Good luck, Genie," she said, "and happy landings."

ack at the B&B, breakfast was over, but the grumbling in Maris's stomach could no longer be ignored. She opened the refrigerator and, to her delight, found that Cookie had saved a chocolate croissant for her.

"Bless you, Cookie," she said quietly.

As she steeped some herbal tea, Maris slowly savored the buttery, flaky pastry. It was an indulgence, to be sure, but how could she turn down home baking from the amazing chef?

She couldn't.

While she sipped her tea, she took a few moments to go over the B&B's to-do list: making the beds, replacing towels, cleaning the bathrooms, and emptying the trash were always at the top. Cookie usually took care of the towels and bathrooms. Maris made the beds and took out the trash.

She polished off the last chocolaty morsel, finished her tea, and loaded her plate into the empty dishwasher. Because she'd already seen the open parking slots outside, she knew that the guests were out and about. Now would be the perfect time to make the beds and take out the trash. Since the B&B was running at less than half occupancy, it took only a matter of a couple hours or so for Maris to complete her chores. She could see that Cookie had finished hers as well, and spied her in the herb garden behind the property. Bear was with her, moving some bags of potting soil.

With the chores done, Maris wandered back to her room, which had once been Aunt Glenda's. As she passed the armoire, her gaze drifted up to her aunt's silk brocade boudoir box. When she'd first arrived back at the B&B, Maris had found her aunt's paperwork in it: insurance policies, the deed to the property, and miscellaneous receipts and warranties. But what had been conspicuous by its absence was a beautiful item from Maris's childhood.

Glenda had possessed a faceted green stone in the shape of an inverted cone. It'd been hung on a delicate silver chain and Maris had always wanted to wear it. But her aunt had told her that it wasn't meant to be worn, because it wasn't a pendant. Instead it was a pendulum.

But when she'd found its small case in the boudoir box, it'd been empty.

Ever since then, she'd wondered where the pendulum had gone, and the occasional bout of nostalgia and curiosity prompted her to search for it again, even though she knew the odds of finding it were slim.

"It has to be *somewhere*," she said.

Over time, she had replaced her aunt's clothes with her own, turning out the pockets before putting them away in storage to make sure the pendulum wasn't tucked away somewhere. But so far, she had turned up nothing. Perhaps it had fallen into some nook or cranny that she just hadn't noticed yet.

Knowing her efforts were probably futile, she pulled the bed away from the wall and glanced behind it before checking the dresser drawers, the back of the armoire, the dressing table, and the nightstand.

Nothing.

Oh well, she thought, putting her hands on her hips. *When it's meant to turn up, it will turn up.*

A familiar meow made her look down to find Mojo looking back up at her.

"Hey there, Mojo," she said, stooping to pick him up.

For a few moments she listened to his contented purring, until she realized he was staring at the wall. Was he watching a spider? But when she followed his gaze, it landed on something that made her frown. Hanging from an empty coat hook near the door was an old, intricate skeleton key.

The key.

She knew all too well where that key led: the basement door in the utility room--the dreaded basement. Maris glanced down at Mojo, raising her eyebrows.

"You think the pendulum is in the basement?" she asked.

He gave her a plaintive, little mew.

"Really?" she said, looking at the key

again. Just the sight of it made her palms damp.

It had almost seemed fated that, during her constant travel from one poorly managed resort to another, she'd eventually get trapped in an elevator. Management had concluded that it was improper maintenance, but no matter the cause, she'd been stuck for three hours without communication or even emergency lighting. She'd considered jumping to reach the ceiling, maybe being able to punch through it and grab something to get out— like they did in the movies. But then she'd worried that landing with a thud after jumping might cause the whole thing to plummet to the ground. In the end she'd opted for standing as still as she could while she screamed for help. Eventually it came. But she'd been slightly claustrophobic ever since.

Mojo still in her arms, Maris squared her shoulders, grabbed the key, and headed across her room to the utility room door. Inside there was a trapdoor on the floor that led to the basement.

Maris shuddered.

Large black hinges matched the heavy

lock and handle. She could already hear the massive tumblers scraping against one another, the sound supplied by her memory. She'd watched Glenda open it many times as a child, and had delighted in running down its dark stairs.

A cold sweat trickled in the small of her back. Nor did it help matters that Mojo had gone rigid and seemed to be glaring at the trapdoor. But more than anything, it was her photographic memory that made her feet feel rooted. She could remember every minute of those three hours in that elevator.

The shrill ring of the cell phone in her pocket made her flinch, as Mojo yowled and leapt to the ground. When she finally managed to take a breath, she yanked out the phone. It was Mac.

"Mac," she exclaimed. "Thank goodness."

There was a pause on the other end before he said, "Ah, hi, Maris. Thank goodness?"

She hurried out of the utility room and let the door close behind her. "Oh, it's just that I was grateful for the distraction," she said quickly. "Not that you're a distraction. I just meant that... Never mind." She took a breath. "What can I do for you?"

"We've caught a break," he said. "We found Edwin Martin's car."

Maris stood still. "Really? Where?"

"You know Jessica Cash at the credit union?" Mac asked.

"Of course," Maris said, remembering the tense exchange between Edwin and Jessica the day he had died. He'd been ordering her around like a personal servant.

"It's parked outside her apartment building." Maris sucked in a breath. "It's been impounded," Mac continued. "Forensics is taking a look at it. But that's not the only reason I'm calling. I've got a search warrant for the clinic."

"Should I meet you there?" Maris asked.

"If you'd like," Mac said. "I could use your...*insight*."

17

Maris parked in front of Inklings New & Used Books which was adjacent to the medical clinic. Three stories tall and four windows wide, the Victorian storefront was white with blue trim and one of the bigger establishments on the Towne Plaza.

The two larger display windows flanking the double doors held paperbacks, hardcovers, and what looked like a collection of antique maps and old photos. It was one of the few places in Pixie Point Bay that Maris had never particularly shopped at. Even as a child, she had been more interested in helping Aunt Glenda, or listening to her records, or playing with the ouija board.

But as it sometimes does, reading had grown on her as she'd gotten older. No matter where she'd had to travel in the world, she found that a book was not just a reliable companion but a respite. Now she found herself eyeing the pretty bookshop from the rental car, wondering if she would be able to sneak in before having to meet Mac. Judging by the fact that his SUV wasn't anywhere in the plaza, she could assume he hadn't arrived yet.

As if on cue, her phone chimed and she fetched it from her purse. It was a text from Mac. He'd run into traffic and was going to be late.

That settles it, she thought, as she grabbed her purse and got out. *It's time for some window shopping.*

She walked up to the display on the left, where there was an arrangement of new releases by authors she recognized as well as ones that were new to her. Of course her favorite books often involved travel to faraway places. Sometimes she'd even been lucky enough to match a book to the spot on the globe where she was working. Fiction or nonfiction, it didn't matter. She'd read anything from memoirs and travelogues to romances and thrillers. Even now she could see a few titles that looked interesting.

But before she went inside, she was drawn to the maps and photos in the other display window. Some of the old photographs were printed on glossy paper, while others had a matte finish. A few were yellowing and tattered around the edges, preserved in plastic sleeves. But upon closer examination, Maris could see that these weren't just any collection of antique images. They were old pictures of the town.

Maris peered in at them and couldn't help but wonder if there might be one of the lighthouse, or Aunt Glenda, or maybe other relatives. Her family had been in Pixie Point Bay for multiple generations. Seeing all the photos of the town and its people, she wondered if it might be nice to frame something genealogical to display at the B&B. She decided to get a closer look.

Inside, the bookstore was as lovely as the outside, and incredibly clean and tidy. Bookshelves with neatly organized books ran the length of the building. Tucked in the corners were shiny wooden tables with comfortable reading chairs arranged around them. Tiffany lamps cast their soft, multi-colored light, giving the place an almost enchanted glow. Potted plants of all shapes and sizes hung from the ceiling, taking advantage of the ample sunlight afforded by the front windows. There was even a tangle of ivy on the back wall. Maris hadn't even thought it was possible to grow ivy indoors. On the front counter, sat a large, glass dispenser of what smelled like apple cider next to a stack of paper cups.

Maris chided herself for not having visited earlier. As she headed towards another arrangement of photos she spotted towards the back, a young Asian woman appeared from one of the aisles.

"Welcome to Inklings," she said, smiling and holding a few books in her arms. "Can I help you find something?"

"Just browsing," Maris said, smiling back at the diminutive woman. With long black hair, and sparkling eyes, she appeared to be in her mid-forties. "I'm just fascinated with these photos you have displayed. Do you have any of the lighthouse? I'm the owner."

"Oh," the woman exclaimed. She set her

books on the nearest shelf and extended a hand. "I'm Minako Page. My husband, Alfred, and I are the owners."

Maris shook her hand. "I'm Maris Seaver. Pleased to meet you."

"Welcome to Pixie Point Bay," Minako said, cheerily. "I don't mind telling you that when Glenda passed away, some folks were worried that would be the end of the B&B. Or worse, that it would be bought up by developers and turned into some kind of mega-resort. With a property like that, it wouldn't surprise me." She picked up the books again. "Anyway, it's nice to see it stay in the family."

"I appreciate you saying that," Maris told her, as they walked to the other photo display.

Minako turned to the pictures. "I don't think we have any of the lighthouse on display right now, but undoubtedly there are some in storage."

"How'd you manage to track them down? Some of them look ancient."

"I was an archivist in another life," Minako replied, "and archives are forever, as they say." She laughed a little. "I find myself researching all manner of Pixie Point Bay history. But it's more of a hobby now."

"No kidding," Maris said. "That sounds fascinating." She gestured to the photos. "And it makes for a wonderful display."

"Alfred seems to think so," Minako replied, her eyes smiling.

One photo in particular jumped out at Maris. It was of a Victorian storefront marked "Klaas's Glass." In front of the store stood a man who was...Kristofer Klaas. Although the man in the image wore period clothing that included a bowler hat, the face was Kristofer's, right down to the handlebar mustache. Of course it couldn't be him, since he wasn't over one-hundred years old, but the resemblance was nothing short of astonishing.

She was just about to ask Minako about it, when there was movement outside the store, in the corner of her eye. Mac's SUV was pulling up outside the medical clinic.

"I'm afraid I've got to go," she told the store owner. "But you have a lovely shop, and I'll most definitely be back. It was nice to meet you."

"Nice to meet you too," Minako said, inclining her head, before Maris headed to the door.

By the time Maris made it out to the front of the medical clinic, Mac was already standing outside.

"Maris," he said, his expression brightening. "I hope you haven't been waiting long. I got detoured around construction."

Maris shook her head, happy to see him. "Not at all. I was just browsing that wonderful bookstore."

Mac looked over her shoulder at it for a moment before he said, "Shall we go inside?"

Jill was still at the reception desk, typing away at a computer. She looked up when they entered. "Back already, Sheriff?"

"Yes," Mac replied, pulling an envelope out of his jacket. "I have a search warrant for the clinic's medical records." He opened the envelope, pulled out the search warrant, and handed it to her. He waited as she looked it over. When she gazed back up at him, he said, "Can you show us where they are?"

"Sure thing," Jill replied, setting down the paperwork before showing them to a room at the very end of the hall. She pulled the door open to reveal a row of filing cabinets as well as stacks of cardboard boxes. If Maris had to guess, she'd say the complete medical records of everyone in Pixie Point Bay were in here.

Possibly everyone in the county, she thought.

"Whose record are you looking for?" Jill asked.

"Edwin Martin's," Mac replied.

"Of course," Jill said. She looked from one filing cabinet drawer to the next, reading their labels. Finally she crouched down and pulled out the bottom drawer of one. "Let's see," she said to herself. "M, A, R..." Her fingers walked across the tops of the different colored folders, and stopped on one in particular. "Martin," she said, and pulled it out with a small grunt from the tightly packed drawer. She stood and handed it over to Mac.

"That should have everything: immunizations, visit notes, prescriptions, the works."

"Great," Mac said, taking it. For a moment, there was an awkward pause.

"Right," Jill said quickly. "I'll let you get to it. Let me know if there's anything else you need."

"Thank you," Mac said and began to rifle through the manilla folder. When the door closed, he said, "What I didn't mention to Nurse Maxwell is that I have the coroner's report. What I'm here to do is corroborate something."

"Oh," Maris said, and waited for him to complete his search. *Corroborate what*, she thought, but let him work in silence.

Finally he stopped, and pulled out one of the papers. "Here it is."

"What does it say?" Maris asked, not bothering to ask what 'it' might be.

Mac read silently for a moment, his gray eyes scanning back and forth over the page. Finally he stopped and closed the folder. "This confirms it."

"Confirms *what*?" Maris replied, about to burst.

"Edwin didn't choke to death on the food

he was eating," Mac replied. "He died of anaphylaxis."

"An allergic reaction?" she asked, surprised. "Are people allergic to grapes?"

"It's a rare allergy, from what I've been told," the sheriff said. "I think it's more likely that it was a reaction to something *on* the grapes."

"Any idea what Edwin *was* allergic to?" Maris asked.

"According to Dr. Rossi," Mac said, running a finger down the page and stopping. "Shellfish, according to this allergy test." He looked up at her. "The coroner found traces of seafood protein in his stomach, along with high histamine levels. That points to an allergic reaction. The thing is, none of the food at the credit union tested positive for those proteins."

"That points to the grapes," Maris said. "Whoever killed Edwin must have done something to them and then disposed of them."

"Exactly," Mac agreed.

"It can't have been easy to live in a place like Pixie Point Bay with a shellfish allergy,"

Maris remarked, glancing back down at the coroner's report.

"According to this, Edwin didn't develop the allergy until he was an adult," Mac said. "It was a recent thing. Which the coroner said can happen sometimes—a person developing an allergy later in life."

"I see," Maris said, frowning. There'd been no hint of shellfish of any sort at the credit union that day. Had he eaten something earlier?

Mac folded up the medical file with the coroner's report inside. "I've got to go over to Jessica Cash's apartment building."

"You don't actually think Jessica had something to do with this, do you?" Maris asked him. As nasty as Edwin had been to the young teller that day, she couldn't imagine her being the mastermind behind his... Allergic reaction? Poisoning?

He tucked the folder under his arm. "Frankly, my gut says no," he said. "But I don't get to make that call. Edwin Martin's car was found at her building. I'm going to question all of the residents about their whereabouts at the time of the hit-and-run, not just her. It's plain old fashioned police work."

"Well, good," Maris said, as he went to the door, "I'm glad she's not a primary suspect."

Mac opened the door and held it for her. "We can choose either to approach our fellow human beings with suspicion," he said, "or to approach them with an open mind, a dash of optimism and a great deal of candor."

Maris looked sideways at him. "More Robert Burns?"

Mac smiled at her. "Tom Hanks."

19

———————

Maris made the short car trip from downtown Pixie Point Bay to the lighthouse, a pretty journey under any circumstance, but particularly now as dappled sunlight filtered through the oaks that lined the road. Maybe it was the vintage photos at the bookstore, or that she was returning to her own Victorian home, but somehow she had the distinct feeling of traveling back in time. The drive and its lush views of the green countryside had probably changed little, even from an era when cars had not been commonplace. By the time Maris parked at the B&B she felt as if she'd traveled lightyears from the town.

As usual for this time of day, the house was empty and Cookie was out in the back.

Maris found her among the patch of herbs that she tended as if it were her child.

"Maris," Cookie said, looking up from her digging and dusting the dirt off her hands. "Where are you coming from?"

"The medical clinic," Maris replied. "The sheriff asked me to meet him there. He had some more information about Edwin Martin."

"Oh?" Cookie said, raising a hand to shield her eyes from the sun.

"It turns out he didn't choke on grapes," Maris said. "He died from an allergic reaction."

"Good heavens," Cookie said, dropping her hand. "It must have been a severe allergy. What was he allergic to?"

"Shellfish," Maris said, and paced down the side of the herb patch.

Cookie gave a low whistle. "Must have made eating out pretty hard in Pixie Point Bay."

"That's what I said," Maris agreed, turning around and walking back to where she'd started. "But it turns out it's an allergy that came on recently."

"Ah," Cookie said. She bent over and

pulled out a little weed, tossing it in a pail as she straightened up. "I guess that would explain it."

"They also found Edwin Martin's car," Maris said, striding down a different side of the garden. "At the apartment building where Jessica Cash—the teller from the credit union—lives."

"So the facts are adding up," Cookie said, watching her. "That all sounds good."

"Except none of it really fits," Maris said, pacing back. "We have a stolen car, a doctor in a coma, a shellfish allergy but nothing that ties it all together. And now Jessica Cash is in the mix, but why would she want Dr. Rossi dead? Even if she had, why would she be foolish enough to park the car outside her apartment building? She didn't strike me as particularly unintelligent."

Cookie picked up her small gardening spade. "Sometimes people in turmoil don't think straight."

Maris had been about to respond when she glimpsed some movement in the house. It looked like Kristofer Klaas had returned. "There's Kristofer," she said, and turned on her heel.

"Hold on a minute," Cookie said. "Just stop right there."

Startled, Maris turned back to her. "What?" she said, and looked around.

"What's the sudden hurry?" the chef and gardener asked.

Maris blinked. "Hurry? I'm not in a hurry." Then she glanced over her shoulder. "I just had a question for Kristofer."

Cookie sighed, tossing the trowel to the dirt. "Have you sat still for even one minute today?"

Maris was surprised all over again. "Sat still?"

Cookie beckoned her closer. "Humor me," she said, with a little smile. "Come on." Maris cocked her head at the diminutive gardener but obliged. "Take a look at this little plant that you've walked past about four times now." She pointed to a few bunches of pink and white flowers. "That's Valerian. It helps with insomnia. This," she continued, indicating a cluster of delicate white flowers with yellow centers, like small daisies, "is chamomile. It's used for relaxation and composure." She deftly plucked a single flower and offered it to Maris. "Take a pinch and tell me what you smell."

I'll smell chamomile, Maris thought but she took the flower.

"Pinch it, close your eyes, and sniff," Cookie said.

It was a good thing Maris had to close her eyes, since it stopped the eye-roll. But when she pinched one of the small leaves and brought it to her nose, it wasn't what she'd expected. Eyes still closed, she frowned a little. It smelled sweet and, if she wasn't mistaken, there was a hint of fruit. Maybe apple? Yes, that was it. It had the faint scent of a Fuji apple.

When she slowly opened her eyes, she looked down at the group of white flowers. They looked so simple and yet their fragrance was incredibly complex. A warm breeze rustled them, wafting what looked like yellow dust into the air. Maris watched it drift toward the lighthouse and, when she lost sight of it, she imagined it carried out to the sea beyond. There it might travel the world, across the bay and then the ocean, taking a small bit of Cookie's herb garden with it.

Maris took in a deep breath and slowly let it go.

When she turned to Cookie, she wasn't there. She'd moved to the other side of the patch of herbs and was tossing another weed in the bucket. As though she'd heard her name called, she looked up at Maris.

"Thank you," Maris said quietly, knowing she wouldn't be heard.

But Cookie understood all the same. "Your welcome," she mouthed.

20

"Maris, there you are," Kristofer said when she arrived in the living room.

He was sitting in one of the overstuffed armchairs making notes in what looked like a day-planner. But when he saw her, he reached into his jacket pocket.

"Good afternoon, Kristofer," she said, watching as he pulled a small, light green mouse from his pocket.

Except it wasn't a green mouse, it was more like a crocheted ball with big ears, a long tail of twisted yarn, and three black dots for the eyes and nose. It was absolutely adorable.

He held it out to her. "I couldn't find

Mojo, but I got this for him." He dropped it in her outstretched hand.

"How cute," she exclaimed. "He's going to love it." It was so soft that it seemed more like a toy for a baby, which only made it better. "Thank you, Kristofer. I'll give it to him the next time I see him. Normally at this time of day he's in need of his *siesta*."

Kristofer grinned. "Aren't we all."

The lifting of his bristly mustache reminded Maris of the bookstore. "You know, I wanted to mention a photo that I saw today that you might want to see."

"A photo?" he said, leaving his pencil in the fold of the day-planner.

"This is going to sound crazy," she said, "but I could've sworn I saw you today. It was in a Victorian photograph on display at Inklings New & Used Books. The man in the picture looked identical to you—except for the turn of the century clothing. It was uncanny. And he ewas standing outside a store called Klaas's Glass."

Kristofer chuckled. "Well, I wish I could say I looked good for my ancient age, but that would've been my grandfather, Karl Klaas. He started the business seventy-five years ago, after he came over from Estonia. He and my father taught me everything I know."

Maris nodded, smiling. "Of course. It had to be something like that." She paused for a moment. "So your family had a storefront in the Towne Plaza, once upon a time?"

His smile disappeared. "To be honest, that's a bit of a sore point."

Maris frowned sympathetically. "I'm sorry to hear that. Care to vent your spleen?"

He shrugged, but ran his hand through his hair. "I vented it years ago. But if you're curious, you'll hear the story in town, so you might as well hear it from me." He looked at both his hands before setting them in his lap. "I'm a good glazier. My family saw to that. But I'm not the most...astute business man."

Maris took a seat opposite him. "I'm sure you do very well," she countered. "You seem very busy."

He tilted his head a little. "Sure. I'm fine with working for myself, but running a brick and mortar, with employees, and everything that entails? Well, I just don't have the head for it." He looked out the window for several moments, and Maris wondered if he was remembering the old days. Then, he seemed to snap out of his reverie. "That guy who died a few days ago, Edwin Martin, he gave me a business loan a while back. I wasn't sure about it, but he gave me the hard sell when I came in to the credit union to make a withdrawal. He said it would help me expand the business, triple my number of clients in the next year. He didn't mention the balloon payment..." He grimaced. "The business, my grandfather's business, ended up being seized."

"The whole business?" Maris asked, eyes wide. The thought of losing a family business hit close to home.

Kristofer sighed. "The building and all the assets. The machinery, the glass, the tools, everything."

Just like Dr. Rossi's house, Maris thought. *How awful.*

"So that's why there's a photo of a glass shop on the plaza with my name on it," he said, picking up his pencil. "And that's also why I won't miss Edwin Martin in the least."

"Do you think he did it on purpose?" Maris asked.

Kristofer pressed his lips into a thin line.

"In my mind, there's no doubt. Good riddance to him, I say. A snake in a suit."

Maris saw her opportunity. "A snake that maybe needed to be killed, would you say?"

He'd been about to make a note in the planner and looked up in puzzlement. But as understanding dawned, he laughed, surprising her.

"If this glazier had wanted to kill him, he'd have put a shard of glass through his heart. Besides, I wasn't in town when it happened. I was on my way from one job to another."

Likely on the road without a witness, she thought.

He smiled at her. "I can see your mind going." He looked back down at his planner, smiling. "Submit my name to the authorities, if you like. I wouldn't mind in the least. It'll only boost my credibility."

21

———

The following morning, while Cookie was getting breakfast ready, Maris decided to call Mac from the lighthouse. She'd wrestled all evening with whether or not to tell him about Kristofer's history with Edwin Martin. Even as she climbed the tower, she went back and forth.

After all, a man who would bring Mojo a cute toy was no murderer. He'd also seemed to enjoy the Wine Down as much as ever. But the glazier no longer lived in Pixie Point Bay, and visited the B&B only a few times a year. The chances that it was coincidence that he'd been in the region when the credit union manager had been killed were good, but not one-hundred percent.

As she exited into the glass room at the

top, she paused for a moment to catch her breath. Just above her, Claribel's brilliant beam rotated, slicing through the fog. Down below the thick mist made the rocky coast barely visible. A lone seagull glided past, heading inland. By the time it disappeared, Maris's breathing had slowed. She dialed Mac.

"Hi, Maris," he said, answering on the second ring. It amazed her how he always sounded so chipper. As the only law officer for miles in every direction, he must have a lot on his plate. Maybe that's why he didn't mind including her in the investigation.

"Good morning," she said, "I have some new information."

"Already? About Edwin Martin?" he asked, immediately interested. "What have you got?"

"You know Kristofer Klaas?" Maris asked.

"The glass guy?" Mac said. "I know of him, but we've never met."

She decided to skip the photo in the bookshop and get right to the interesting part. "His shop was repossessed by the credit union. It had been in his family for three generations."

"Oh really," Mac said. "Interesting."

"Apparently Edwin pressured Kristofer into accepting a loan with a balloon payment."

"Ouch," Mac said. "I'm getting the sense that more people wanted Edwin Martin dead than alive."

"Me too," she agreed, and realized that was really the reason she'd called. She didn't think Kristofer was capable of killing someone, glass shard or not. But an image of Edwin Martin was forming that wasn't particularly rosy.

"How did you come across this information?" the sheriff asked.

"Kristofer is staying at the B&B while he's working in the region and, after he gave me a toy for Mojo, he told me all about it."

Mac laughed a little. "A suspect who gives toys to cats."

"I know," Maris said, smiling, relieved that Mac was seeing it the way she was. "Not exactly a prime suspect."

"I appreciate it all the same," he said. "On this end, forensics got nothing from the car, as expected. But after the coroner's report about the anaphylaxis, I've got a search warrant for the credit union. I'll be heading there shortly if you'd like to join me."

"Absolutely," Maris answered quickly. "I just need to take care of a few things here, then I'll head over."

"Great," he said. "See you then."

They ended the call, and Maris hurried down to the house. She was on her way past the parlor when she caught a glimpse of fluffy black fur. She stopped, backpeddled a few steps, and paused. Mojo was on the ouija board, his fur standing up, and a distant look in his big orange eyes. His soft triangular ears were swiveling like radar dishes and, for all the world, it looked like he was listening to something.

Slowly he sat down on the board and, as Maris watched in amazement, he settled a front paw on the planchette. With a movement that looked deliberate, he pushed it just a little ways until it stopped. Maris quickly stepped over and looked through the plastic window to see what he might spell. But the planchette hadn't landed on a letter. It was the small drawing of the sun.

"The sun?" she asked him softly. "Is it something about the time of day? Is that it?"

But in response, the little cat simply blinked his eyes, shook out his fur, and jumped to the ground. On his way out of the room, he stopped to pick up the new yarn mouse from Kristofer. Then without so much as a glance over his shoulder, he bounced out of the room and disappeared.

Maris threw her hands in the air and then shrugged. "Thanks," she called after him.

In the kitchen she found Cookie setting up the warming trays.

"Hey Cookie," Maris said. "I've got to go into town to meet the sheriff. Need anything?"

"Yes, actually," the chef said, raising a finger. "I'm glad you asked. I'd like to spruce up the pancakes tomorrow morning for the Longacre girls. Would you be a dear and pick up some semi-sweet chocolate morsels?"

"You've got it," replied Maris. "I'll grab lunch while I'm out, too."

22

As Maris pulled up outside the credit union once again, she could see the sheriff through the front room window. It looked like he was searching Edwin's desk in the corner.

When she entered, she saw that he wasn't alone. Standing off to the side behind their desks were Ashley Pound and Jessica Cash, the latter looking worried and a bit frazzled.

"Hi, Jessica," she said, smiling to the two women. "Ashley."

"Ms. Seaver," Ashley, the short brunette, said, returning her smile. "I'm surprised to see you back here so soon."

"Actually," Maris replied, "I'm here to meet the sheriff."

"Ah," Ashley said, "Well, you've found him."

Jessica had yet to acknowledge or even look at her. Instead she was staring at Mac performing his search.

"I wonder," Maris said to Ashley quietly. "If you could show me where the glasses are in the kitchen?"

When Ashley gave her a quizzical look, Maris nodded subtly in the direction of that room and headed that way.

Though Ashley paused for a moment, she said, "Sure, you bet," and followed.

When the kitchen door closed, Maris turned to the young teller. "Let me just be clear that I'm trying to help Jessica. But you're under no obligation to answer my questions."

Ashley considered for a second. "I'd like to help Jessica too. I know that Mr. Martin's car was found at her apartment building." She glanced at the door and lowered her voice. "What is it that you want to know?"

Maris leaned in and said quietly. "It was obvious to me that there was some, shall we say, tension between Jessica and Mr. Martin. Do you know why?"

"Take this with a grain of salt," Ashley

said, "because I just overheard it. Okay?" Maris nodded, and Ashley continued. "It was a while ago, maybe three or four months. I was heading to the closet to get a new roll of paper for my adding machine, but then I heard Jessica yelling."

Maris cocked her head at the teller. "From inside the closet?"

"That's right," Ashley said. "Then I heard a loud slapping sound. At the time, I wasn't sure what it was, so I pulled the door open. I thought maybe she'd fallen, or knocked something down from one of the shelves. Anyway, as soon as I opened the door, Mr. Martin stormed out. There was a bright red handprint on his cheek."

Maris's eyes narrowed and she felt anger begin to burn in her chest. "Any idea what happened between them?"

"No," Ashley said, shaking her head. "Jessica came out sobbing a minute later and ran to the bathroom. I tried to ask her what happened, but she wouldn't tell me. Still, I think it's pretty obvious."

"He was harassing her and she rejected him," Maris said, her voice tight.

"Exactly," Ashley agreed. "And ever since

then, he made a point to make her wait on him hand and foot. It was always something menial and inconvenient, and no matter how many times I offered to help, he forced her to be the one to do it."

"So you think he was getting back at her for rebuffing him?"

"I'm almost positive," Ashley replied. She put her hand on Maris's arm. "Please don't tell anyone, though. She's upset enough as it is."

"It's all right," Maris reassured her.

By the time they returned to the front, Mac had moved on to Jessica's desk. She was standing in front of it, watching his every movement, and biting one of her already distressed looking nails. Ashley went to her, put a comforting arm around her shoulders, and murmured something to her.

Behind them two customers came in, brought up short by the sight of Mac behind one of the desks.

"Do you want me to take them, Jessica?" Ashley asked.

"No," the blonde teller said, taking a shaky breath. "No, it's okay. I can do it."

They each greeted a customer and escorted them in—Ashley to her desk and Jessica to a coffee table in the small waiting area.

Maris approached Mac. "Hey," she said, watching as he rummaged in a drawer.

"Hey," Mac said, not looking up.

"So what is it you're looking for?" she asked. Out of the corner of her eye, she saw Jessica shoot them an uneasy glance as she went to Mr. Martin's desk and used the cash drawer.

"Nothing in particular," the sheriff replied. "Missing stuff, things that seem out of place, anything that might be useful." His brow furrowed, and he straightened up, an envelope in his hands. He opened it and thumbed through the contents.

"Are those receipts?" Maris asked.

"Gas station," Mac said nodding. "Flour Power... Wait a minute." He frowned, holding up a small sales ticket. She recognized it immediately. It was the type issued by Bertha, the antique cash register at the Main Street Market. It was dated the day before the murder, and on the back was written one word: grapes.

Uh oh, Maris thought.

Mac's face went stony and their conversation died as he watched the two tellers until their customers left. As soon as they were out the door, he approached Jessica, who looked spooked. "Yes, Sheriff?"

"Jessica," Mac said, obviously doing his best to be gentle with the questioning, "would you mind telling me about this receipt?"

He handed her the little paper, and Jessica's eyes almost seemed to bulge. "I, um..." She swallowed. "I mean, that was just a normal shopping trip. I always keep the receipts for the petty cash." She was talking fast. "Mr. Martin was always asking for snacks, especially grapes. Those were his favorites. He started making me pick food up for him, lug the water bottles–"

"Okay," Mac said, motioning for her to slow down. "I get the picture. And when was the last time you bought grapes?"

"I, um..." She bit her nail and looked at the floor. "I can't remember."

Maris didn't like the direction this was headed but was helpless to stop it.

"All right," Mac said, putting the receipt back in the envelope. "Would you know what happened to the grapes Mr. Martin was eating before he died? They disappeared after his death."

"No," Jessica replied in such a small voice that Maris could barely hear her. "I'm sorry." Her lower lip began to tremble.

Still, that didn't stop the next words that the sheriff spoke: "I'm sorry, Jessica, but I'm afraid I'm going to have to ask you to come with me to the station. I'm placing you under arrest for the murder of Edwin Martin."

23

Chocolate chips, Maris told herself for the tenth time as she pulled up outside the Main Street Market. After the startling and unwelcome events at the credit union, it would be like her to forget the chocolate chips *and* lunch. The truth was that—despite the car, the receipt, and the motive—she just couldn't see Jessica as a killer.

Inside the market, Howard waved to her from behind the front counter as Maris made a bee line to the baking section. Finding chocolate was a superpower of hers, and within seconds she had the bag of semi-sweet morsels in hand. But on her way back to the front of the store, she made a point of looking for Bryan.

He was in the refrigerated section again, loading what looked like jumbo shrimp into the case. "Hey, Bryan," she said.

"Oh, hey, Ms. Seaver," Bryan replied, looking up from his work.

Although he was wearing rubber gloves, Maris could see a bit of white gauze peeking out. "How's your hand?"

"It's pretty good," he said, flexing his fingers. "It only needed a few stitches. And I'm still able to work, so..." He shrugged. "It could be worse, I guess."

"And how are *you* doing?" she asked.

For a moment he seemed surprised by the question, but then his shoulders sagged. "I'm okay," he said. "You know..."

Although he was far from his smiling self, he also seemed to be eating and had good color. But she also knew that the shock of it all might yet to have really hit home.

"In fact," Maris said, "I do know something about losing a loved one when you're young." When he stared at the floor, she continued, "So if you ever need an ear to bend, you know where to find me." He nodded. "And by that, I mean the chocolate aisle," she added, hefting the bag of morsels and trying to coax a smile from him, but he just looked at her feet.

"All right," Maris said quietly. It looked like a career in standup wouldn't be happening any time soon. "I don't want to keep you from your work. Or cause another accident. I'll see you later."

"See you later, Ms. Seaver," Bryan said, turning back to his task.

As Maris made her way back to the front of the store she found that her homing instinct had brought her down the candy, peanuts and popcorn aisle. Her feet came to a slow stop opposite the candy bar section. Howard kept an excellent assortment on hand. All of her favorites were here: the crispy wafers, the almond and coconut, and the peanut, caramel, and nougat. Maybe she ought to keep one in the car for emergencies. But even as the thought crept into her mind, so did the digital readout on the scale. She took a step back.

The only emergency she had to worry about was not being able to fit into her clothes. She strode away without looking back.

When Maris arrived at the counter, she

could see Howard wiping down the screen of the new digital checkout system. "I see Bryan convinced you to replace the cash register," she remarked as she set the chocolate chips down. "I was wondering if you'd actually go through with it."

"Sure did," replied Howard. "Isn't she beautiful? I'm thinking of calling her Gertie. Or maybe Patricia. What do you think?"

"She looks more like a Maude to me," Maris replied, eyeing the computer.

"Maude," mused Howard as he rang her up. "Yeah, I like that. It's a strong name. At any rate, I'm glad I took the plunge. You're never too old to learn new tech, and the boy's enough of a wizard that he had the thing up and running in under an hour, if you can believe it."

"I can," Maris said. She glanced over her shoulder, where she could still see Bryan. He had moved to the frozen cases and was methodically stacking boxed microwave dinners. "How's he holding up?" she asked quietly. "I mean, not just from the injury, but from everything else."

"I think he's doing well," Howard replied. "I've offered to let him take some time off, but he keeps insisting it's no trouble. Bryan's a hard worker, no doubt. He didn't even file a workers' comp request after that little pickle accident, even when I suggested he should. I guess he must not have been hurt that badly." Howard smiled at her as he reached into one of the jars behind the counter and offered Maris a familiar striped candy stick. "Barber pole for the little lady?"

Though Maris knew she'd have to save this for another—weight reduced—time, she smiled as she accepted the stick. "Thank you, Howard."

24

Maris surveyed the Towne Plaza and considered what to pick up for lunch, when she suddenly recalled her precognitive vision. Although she might have expected to see events at the credit union, she'd seen a certain restaurant instead. This would be the perfect opportunity to visit Delia's Smokehouse.

After stowing the morsels in her car, Maris decided to leg it over to the smokehouse, across the Towne Plaza. She passed the red oriental gazebo, and in minutes was outside the restaurant. Pushing open the big red door, Maris was immediately and pleasantly struck by the smell of the grill. The scent of spices like paprika, chili, and pepper was mixed with the sweet smell of brown sugar.

Maris also noted with some satisfaction that it was exactly as it had been in her vision. The long, roughly hewn plank tables were flanked by simple wooden chairs filled by a moderately sized crowd. At the left of the giant dining area was the wood counter with its padded brown leather stools. At the right was the steel salad bar, and the open kitchen beyond it. Over the center of the entire room hung a giant wagon wheel with flickering electric candles.

A loud rumbling erupted from Maris's stomach, but thankfully no one was close enough to hear. She picked up a menu from the rack attached to the hostess stand and started her happy search.

"Maris," said a woman's voice, bringing her attention up. "It's good to see you."

Delia Burnside was a plump woman of forty, with a head of tight red curls and dancing hazel eyes. She never seemed to be in anything other than a jovial mood, and was the culinary genius behind the restaurant. A transplant from somewhere in the Southwest, her smoking abilities made her a hot commodity. Her award-winning recipes often drew hungry tourists from the whole region and beyond.

"Delia," Maris answered, smiling. "Good to see you too."

The chef set a stack of folded menus into the rack. "You're still in town."

Maris grinned at her. "I've decided to stay."

"Well," Delia said, smiling back, "that's the best news I've heard all day. So what kept you away from the smokehouse for so long? It's not my cooking, is it?"

Maris had to laugh "Oh far from it," she said. "It's the battle of the bulge that I've been waging. It keeps me pretty close to the vegetable and fruit aisles." *And the candy counter*, she thought, with just the slightest twinge of guilt.

"Don't eat too much of that healthy stuff," Delia said. "Men like ladies with some meat on their bones." She gave her a little wink. "Kind of like good home barbecue."

Maris grinned, just as Delia's father approached from behind the wood counter.

"Well I'll be peppered," he said, his thick

white mustache curving up with his smile. "If it isn't Maris."

Maybe a little more stout and quite a bit grayer than his daughter, Eugene Burnside nevertheless had the same buoyant personality. Now that Delia had taken over the business, he mostly waited tables. He was carrying a platter loaded down with empty plates and used utensils, but the weight of it didn't seem to bother him. It certainly didn't stop him from making a detour to them.

"How are things going at the old B&B?" he asked.

"Not too bad," Maris replied. "We've got a few guests right now, not full up, but not too empty either. I was just in town to pick up some supplies."

"Ah," Eugene said, "so you decided to stop by for lunch?"

"I was actually hoping to get some take-out," Maris replied. "I'm thinking maybe four barbecue sandwiches."

"Good choice," Delia said, nodding her approval. "Good for takeout too. Which sandwich did you have in mind?"

"The salmon, I think," Maris said. "The menu said it's locally caught."

"By Slick Duff himself," Delia said, "I'm happy to say. I'll put the order in right now." With that, she took the platter of empty dishes from her father and bustled off in the direction of the kitchen.

"Superb sandwiches," Eugene said, turning to her. "Between you and me, that's the best thing on the menu."

"Oh really?" Maris asked. "The barbecue salmon sandwich?"

Eugene nodded. "I've always been a fish guy myself, but there's something in Delia's seasoning that just knocks it out of the park."

"Well," Maris replied, "I guess that would explain why every time I pick it up, my cat goes wild for it."

"Mojo?" he asked, which made Maris grin as she wondered if more people knew her cat than her.

"It's like he can smell it even before I open the car door," she said. "But—and here's the strangest part—he never does it when I bring fish home from the market."

"Oh, well, that's an easy one," Eugene replied. "That's because fresh fish doesn't smell." Seeing her perplexed look, Eugene leaned in close, lowering his voice. "Here's an industry secret for you. Seafood only smells after it's been cooked, smoked, or brined—or when it's gone bad."

Maris blinked. "I always thought fresh fish was supposed to smell like...well, fish, I guess."

"Spoken like someone who hasn't been shown," Eugene said. "Don't worry, you're not alone. Be right back."

Before Maris had time to ask what he was doing, Eugene was hurrying off in the direction of the kitchen, leaving her to wait by the hostess stand. She idly perused the menu again, and picked up a couple of paper ones she could take back to the B&B. When she looked up, Eugene was making his way back. In one hand was a plastic bag of gray, raw shrimp and in the other a plate of plump, white and pink, skewered shrimp.

His smile was extra broad. "First, shrimp from the barbie," he said, handing the plate to her. "Take a whiff."

As Maris did, she found her mouth watering. It was the most scrumptious shrimp she'd ever smelled, something like a cross between the mildest fish and a slight charcoal scent.

"Wonderful," she said, passing it back.

He gave her the bag. "Slick brought these in last night. Caught them yesterday. Take a whiff. Go ahead."

Normally Maris wouldn't be sticking her nose in a bag of raw *anything*, but Eugene had gone to the trouble of trying to educate her. So she brought the bag to her nose and took a tentative sniff. She frowned a little. There was no smell at all. She opened the bag wider, and took a good inhale. Again, there was simply no scent to it.

"That's..." she said, just as a thought occurred to her, "...amazing." She looked from the bag to the plate, and back again.

"Maris," Eugene said, watching her. "Are you all right?"

"Never better," she said. "I'm going to step outside and make a quick call."

25

"I'm sorry, Maris," Mac said, sounding confused on the other end of the phone. "You want me to do *what*?"

"I know," Maris replied, "It sounds crazy, I agree." In fact the more she thought about it, the crazier it seemed.

She was pacing outside of the smoke-house, not thinking about the barbecue anymore. Eugene had seemed confused when she'd excused herself, but the look on her face must have told him something. He hadn't followed her out to the sidewalk or brought her order to her.

"Maris," Mac said, sounding every bit the voice of reason. "It's a bit of a, shall we say, an unusual request."

Maybe he was right. Maybe she was kidding herself.

"I know," she said, rubbing the back of her neck. Her mind was moving so fast that she was having a hard time keeping her thoughts straight—let alone articulating them. "It's hard to explain why. I'm not sure I really know myself. But they can hardly refuse a request from you." There was only silence on the other end. "Besides, what do you have to lose?" She stopped her pacing and listened intently.

There was another pause, but then he said, "Since it's almost lunchtime, I'm not sure if I'll be able to reach everyone. But I'll give it a try."

"Thank you, Mac," Maris said, sighing with huge relief.

"Don't thank me yet," he said. "What time are you thinking?"

She glanced inside the restaurant to see Eugene leaving her to-go order on the hostess stand. "Maybe a couple of hours?" It'd be just enough time to get the sandwiches home.

"All right," he said.

She headed to the restaurant door. "Great, I've got to–"

"Hold on," he said quickly, stopping her. "Don't hang up just yet." She heard some rustling of the phone as though it was being repositioned. "Let me get a pencil and paper." She waited for a few moments. "Okay. What were those names again?"

MARIS HAD ONLY JUST HUNG up with Mac when her phone rang. She stared at the screen.

"Miami?" she muttered, recognizing the prefix for the Luguan Imperial Resorts headquarters. Had something happened to Genie?

"Hello," she said, "this is Maris Seaver."

"Good afternoon, Maris," said a woman's voice. "This is Pam Watson."

Maris pressed her lips into a firm line. "Pam, how nice to hear from you," she lied.

"How is life treating you in...Pixel Bay?"

Maris's teeth ground a little. "Pixie Point Bay," she corrected. "Life is treating me well."

"That's good to hear," Pam said, no doubt also lying. There was a pause. "Shall we cut to the chase?"

Maris gripped her phone tightly. "I'd say that'd be prudent."

"I'm offering you Geneva Tharald's job, including a signing bonus, a relocation package, and six weeks off per year."

Maris's mouth fell open and for several seconds she couldn't speak.

"Maris," Pam said, "are you still there?"

"Yes, I'm still here," Maris said, ready to throw the phone into the plaza. "And here is where I'm staying."

"You haven't heard about the bonus," Pam said, sounding smug.

"Listen to me," Maris said, squeezing her eyes shut. "*And hear me*. There is nothing on this earth that could make me take that job. If there's anyone who deserves that bonus, it's Genie. She'll need it for the day when *she's* burned out, when *her* health is on the line, and *she* is done."

"Maris, you're one of a kind," Pam said, her tone unemotional. "I'm willing to put a very high value on your uniqueness."

That tore it.

"Pam, my best advice to you is to stop seeing people as paychecks. If you can manage to see them as people and treat them as people, then you won't have to hear the following."

Maris hit the call end button. Then she blocked that number.

26

—————

Maris took the sandwiches directly to the back of the property, down the side of the B&B to where she suspected her lunch companions were working. Sure enough, Bear was following Cookie and pushing a wheelbarrow of soil.

Maris waved at them. "Hey, you two." She lifted the to-go bag in her other hand. "Lunch is on."

As they joined her on the porch, Maris laid the sandwiches out on the table: one each for Cookie and her, and two for Bear. Although he sat down with her, Cookie paused and looked down at her grimy fingers.

"I've had my hands in the dirt all morning," she said. "I'm going to go wash up." She headed to the back porch door. "Don't wait for me," she called to them over her shoulder.

Somehow Maris's growling stomach had given way to butterflies. Only now did it occur to her that the sheriff did have something to lose. This scheme of hers wouldn't just be a waste of time. He was risking his stature in the community—at the very least the opinion of others—if she wasn't right.

"Aren't you hungry, Maris?" Bear asked.

He'd politely been waiting for her to start. "Oh, um, sure," she said, unwrapping her sandwich. She watched as his thick fingers worked nimbly to undo the paper and foil.

"It looks good," he said, smiling. "Thank you."

"My pleasure," she said, distractedly.

Maybe she ought to call Mac and cancel the whole thing. After all, who was she? She glanced up at the lighthouse. She was the Pixie Point Bay lightkeeper and B&B owner —not an officer of the law.

"Why don't you eat?" Bear asked.

It was a simple enough question. But the real answer made her put her chin in her hand as she gazed out to the tranquil bay, and the immense ocean beyond it.

"I think I'm doing the right thing," she said, almost to herself, "but I'm not sure if I'm the one who should be doing it."

"Isn't doing the right thing," Bear said, "always the right thing to do?"

It took her a moment to process what he'd said. Maris cocked her head a little, and turned to look at him. "I'm sorry, what did you say?"

He swallowed, then used a napkin to wipe his mouth and beard. "Isn't doing the right thing, always the right thing to do?"

She stared at him, and managed to keep her mouth from dropping open. His gentle brown eyes looked into hers as if he was expecting an answer to his honest question.

"Yes," she finally said. "It is."

Satisfied, he went back to work on his sandwich, just as Cookie rejoined them. "What have we got for lunch?" she asked, taking a seat.

Maris smiled at Bear. "Philosophy 101, it turns out." She picked up her barbecue salmon, and took a nice, healthy bite.

27

In the Towne Plaza of Pixie Point Bay, the warm sun had begun its descent to the horizon. For what felt like the hundredth time in the last few days, Maris parked near the credit union. Before she'd left the B&B, Cookie had said to be careful of the ruts she'd created between there and here. But if Maris was right about what she suspected, this could be the last trip to the credit union she'd need to make for a while.

As she got out and shut the car door, she could see a light on inside, and when she reached the sidewalk, Maris also caught sight of the sheriff. He was standing near Edwin's desk. Bryan was inside already too, sitting on the couch in the small waiting area. Of course the two tellers were there as well. Although Jessica wasn't wearing an orange jumpsuit, Maris knew that Mac must have brought her from a jail cell.

"Maris Seaver," said a voice from behind her. "You really do have a flair for the dramatic."

She turned to face Millicent Leclair, unable to keep from smiling at the sight of the old woman moving quickly in her direction. Her enormous crochet supply bag was tucked under one arm and her black eyes danced with excitement.

"Millicent," Maris said, "glad you could make it."

"Are you joking?" Millicent said, touching her lightly on the arm as she came to a stop on the sidewalk. "There's no way I would miss something as thrilling as this." She leaned in towards Maris, her voice taking on a conspiratorial tone. "You know who did it, don't you?" she asked. "Wait until the ladies at the crochet club hear about this. They're going to be so jealous that I was here to see this all unfold. It's thrilling, I tell you, thrilling!"

Though Maris could see precisely how Millicent would think that, and was glad she did, she also had a notion that not everyone was going to be 'thrilled.' For her part, the butterflies had returned and she'd be glad to see the whole thing over and done.

"Well," she said, "let's hope it lives up to expectations." But as Millicent nearly bounded up the porch steps, Maris decided it couldn't disappoint her. She was already as giddy as a schoolgirl.

Maris managed to get to the door before the older lady, and held it open for her. Millicent hurried into the credit union, giving Maris a wink as she passed and looking like a cat who'd already caught, cooked, and eaten the canary. Maris was just about to follow her inside, when she caught sight of Kristofer Klaas hurrying down the sidewalk. He looked a little agitated, his hair a bit messy, and his shirt stained with something that looked like dried glue.

"Sorry, sorry," he huffed through his mustache as he approached. "I had a last minute skylight repair to make," he said, talking fast. "It had to be water tight. I hope I haven't kept the sheriff waiting." Worried, he looked past her. "I've got another customer to get to before this day is over. This won't take long, will it? I'm guessing it's something to do with Edwin Martin. The sheriff didn't say much, just that he had a few things to go over with me." The glazier was almost hyperventilating, and Maris could hardly blame him. Kristofer stared at her for a moment, a wary look in his eyes. "This isn't about the glass business, is it?" he asked. "I know we talked about it the other day, and I know I probably didn't paint myself in the best light, but–"

Maris put up a hand to stop him. "The sooner we start," she said. "The sooner we'll finish. We'll explain everything inside. And thank you for coming. This won't take long." Maris held open the door for him and followed him inside. As all eyes turned to her, she forced herself to stand up tall, pausing just inside to turn the "Open for Business" sign to "Closed."

Kristofer hurried to the opposite side of the room, where he stood by Mac, looking as if he wanted to say something though he kept quiet in the silent room. Bryan Martin had moved to lean against one of the tellers' desks, his hands in his pockets, looking at the floor. Millicent had taken a seat behind Edwin Martin's desk. For some reason that

Maris couldn't fathom, she looked as if she belonged there. Her latest crochet project was spread out in her lap, this one a marvelous-looking beanie in the colors of a sunset.

Jessica and Ashley were in the back of the room near the hallway that led to the kitchen. Jessica was pale, with dark circles under her eyes, and was biting her nail. Ashley had a hand on her shoulder and was rubbing it soothingly, although she looked almost as on-edge as her colleague. Maris saw that Jessica wasn't restrained, and inwardly thanked Mac. He'd already gone above and beyond the call just by bringing her here.

"Sheriff," Ashley said. "I think we'd all like to know what's going on. Is there a reason you've asked all these people to be here?"

Bryan Martin looked up. "If this has something to do with my dad, I'd like to know."

Mac hooked his thumbs in his utility belt and nodded at Maris. "The reason I've asked you all here is something that Maris Seaver is going to have to tell you."

Suddenly, all heads swiveled toward her again. For a moment, it felt like being a bug under a magnifying glass.

Clearing her throat, Maris said, "Thank you all for coming here on such short notice." She clasped her hands in front of her to keep them from trembling. "To answer both of those questions," she continued, "yes. This is about Edwin Martin's murder."

"I don't mean any disrespect here," Kristofer said, "but if this has something to do with the investigation, with the death, then shouldn't...well...Sheriff McKenna be the one talking to us?"

Maris exchanged a look with Mac that silently said, *that question is yours.*

Mac acknowledged the glazier with a tilt of his head. "That's why I'm here, Mr. Klaas. This is part of the investigation—officially." He looked up, and for a moment his gray eyes met Maris's, and she saw confidence there.

"I trust her," Millicent declared. "And if I trust her, then you can trust her."

Maybe it was the fact that she was sitting behind the big desk, or that her voice simply had the ring of authority, but everyone visibly settled down. Millicent returned to her crocheting, and for a moment the only sound in the credit union was the hum of the air conditioning.

Maris stepped a couple of paces further into the room. "I realize that everyone is busy and that the credit union needs to reopen, so I'll keep this brief," she said. She took a deep breath. What she had to say wasn't pleasant, but drawing it out wasn't going to make it any better. "A number of you had reason to dislike Edwin Martin, even possibly to want him dead."

"Wait a minute," Ashley exclaimed, "you think one of us did it?" She looked around at the assembled group. "One of us?"

Mac made a "hold on" motion with his hand, and the teller stopped.

"Kristofer," Maris said, making eye contact with the glazier, "you lost your business because of a predatory loan. A loan that came from this credit union. It was the balloon payment at the end of that loan that caused you to lose a business and building that had been in your family for three generations."

"Of course," Kristofer said, spreading his hands. "I've admitted it. It's probably a matter of public record." He gestured to the bookstore next door, through the wall. "You said yourself that you saw an old photo of the glass shop."

"Exactly," Maris said. "But what isn't a matter of record is the fact that Edwin Martin suggested it to you, even pressured you to take it."

Kristofer's face turned angry. "Look, I don't want to speak ill of the dead..." His eyes flicked to Bryan. "So I guess I'll keep my thoughts to myself."

"Is *that* what happened?" Millicent asked, turning to him. "It happened awfully quick."

Kristofer snapped his fingers. "Like that."

"Millicent," Maris said, "you had been watching Edwin for a while, you and the other ladies in the crochet club. Helen concluded immediately that he'd been murdered as soon as she found out he was dead. It was clear that all of you were certain he was a less than savory individual."

"An understatement," Millicent agreed, still crocheting, "if you'll pardon my being blunt, young man." She looked at Bryan, who only shrugged and looked at the ground. "And I'm not afraid to say it. Ask any of the By

Hook or Crook ladies and they'll tell you the same. We'd had our eye on that one for quite some time."

"Edwin wronged a lot of people," Maris agreed. "You were the one to tell me about Dr. Rossi."

"Dr. Rossi?" Kristofer asked. "What did he do to the doctor?" From the way everyone looked at her, they had the same question.

"Dr. Rossi lost his house and his family when the credit union foreclosed," Maris answered. "It's the lovely home that Edwin lived in at the time of his death."

Millicent tsked and both Jessica and Ashley gasped.

"No doubt Dr. Rossi is just the tip of the iceberg," Maris said and pointedly looked at Jessica, who looked away.

"Tell them, Jessica," Ashley urged her.

The blonde woman looked at her fellow teller. "Are you insane?"

Ashley put her hands on her hips. "You've already been arrested. Just tell them the truth." Ashley put a hand on her arm. "For your own sake. You can't keep it a secret."

Maris waited as Jessica bit her nail, and moved her weight from one foot to the other.

Finally, she went still and looked defiantly at the group. "He sexually harassed me." This time it was Millicent's turn to gasp. "There, I said it."

Ashley patted her shoulder. "I heard you slap him, in the closet."

"Good for you!" Millicent crowed.

"Not really," Jessica replied. "That's when all the demeaning work assignments began."

Maris shook her head. "Even in the brief time I was here to open an account, I saw him treat you with contempt."

Ashley and Jessica both said, "All the time," and had to smile at each other.

"With all due respect," Bryan said, with just a hint of impatience in his voice, "where is this going, Ms. Seaver?"

Maris looked at him. "To be succinct, motive isn't enough to prove murder."

"Then why are we here?" Jessica asked, her voice almost pleading. "We don't even know how he died."

"But we do," Mac replied. "Edwin Martin died of anaphylaxis after eating grapes."

"Anaphylaxis?" Kristofer said, incredulous. "That's like an allergic reaction, right?"

He looked to Mac for confirmation, and the sheriff nodded.

"Interesting," Millicent murmured, not looking up from her crocheting. "Was he allergic to grapes?"

"No," Jessica said, before Maris could reply. "He couldn't have been. He had me buy them all the time. He was always eating them."

"That's right," Maris said. "He wasn't allergic to grapes. Mac, could you tell them about the patch?"

Mac took a few steps forward to address the room. "We found a transdermal patch in Dr. Rossi's possessions after the hit and run that put him in a coma."

"A transdermal patch?" Bryan asked, turning to him.

"Yes," Mac replied. "It's a type of medical patch that delivers medicine through the skin, like the ones you use to quit smoking. But the lab results have come in, and they've confirmed it wasn't nicotine, or scopolamine for seasickness. It was aconitine."

"What's aconitine?" Ashley asked

"It's a kind of poison," Mac replied. "It's

highly toxic. More importantly, it can be absorbed through the skin."

"So does that mean Dr. Rossi killed Edwin?" Millicent asked, looking perplexed.

"No," Maris replied, "although not for lack of trying."

Kristofer crossed his arms over his chest. "But you can't prescribe a patch full of poison."

"After Edwin died," Maris responded, putting her hands behind her back, "Dr. Rossi asked a question about whale watching. It struck me as odd at the time."

Ashley took a step forward. "That's right," she said. "I remember. He asked if Mr. Martin had gone whale watching recently. It was odd because it isn't the right season."

"That's right," Maris said. "There was something strange about Dr. Rossi's behavior the day Edwin Martin died. He seemed to dismiss the grapes out of hand. He seemed confused about them." She pursed her lips. "I think that when Dr. Rossi arrived he initially thought that *he* had murdered Mr. Martin. He had already poisoned the patches, but he hadn't been expecting him to die that quickly. I suspect he rushed here to cover his tracks."

"But as Kristofer says, you can't prescribe poison," Millicent pointed out. She had set down her crochet project, and was eyeing everyone intensely.

"That's where Slick comes in," Maris said. "I had an interesting conversation with him a few nights ago. He came to the lighthouse to talk to me, and said that he had seen something interesting the day after Edwin's murder. He'd seen Dr. Rossi earlier that day aboard Edwin's yacht. He thought it was strange, because he knew that Edwin had died. Eventually he had to help Rossi off the boat, and the doctor couldn't get away fast enough."

"Do you know what he was doing on my dad's yacht?" Bryan asked.

"My theory," Maris answered, "is that he had gone back to retrieve the rest of the poisoned seasickness patches that he had tampered with. He had given them to Edwin not expecting them to be used until whale watching season, but now he had to cover his tracks. Edwin's death wasn't yet being investigated as a murder, so this was his chance to get rid of any evidence of his involvement. The thing he didn't realize, though, was that *he* wasn't the one whose murder plan succeeded."

"So he tried to kill Mr. Martin but didn't succeed," Ashley said, shaking her head. "But if he didn't kill Mr. Martin, then who did?"

The others nodded and everyone's gaze fixed on Maris.

"Without the poison being responsible," she said, "we were back to anaphylaxis and Mr. Martin's shellfish allergy."

"So it *was* an allergic reaction," Kristofer said.

"So to speak," Maris replied. "I mean, in the sense that it was an *induced* allergic reaction."

"The coroner found seafood protein in his stomach," Mac said, "along with the elevated histamine levels."

"You're saying someone gave him seafood without him realizing it?" Ashley asked. She looked around at the group. "I'm sorry, Ms. Seaver, but I find that a little hard to believe."

"That's what I thought at first, too," Maris replied. "But then I had a rather interesting conversation with Eugene Burnside, just earlier this afternoon, in fact," she continued. "He told me that fresh, uncooked seafood, contrary to popular belief, doesn't have a smell. When it's freshly caught, it's completely odorless."

"Meaning?" Jessica asked.

"Meaning," Maris said, "that juice from fresh seafood could have been injected into the grapes that Edwin was eating just before he died, causing the allergic reaction that killed him."

Incredulous looks shot around the room, but Maris could almost see them thinking it through. Eventually a still silence returned.

"It would have to be someone who was familiar with Mr. Martin's eating habits," Maris continued, glancing at Jessica. The teller lowered her gaze. "But there's more to it than that. There were the poisoned grapes, obviously. But whoever killed Edwin also needed a way to get into the credit union when it was closed in order to poison the grapes." Again, Jessica shrank, but Maris pressed on. "I realize that this all points to Jessica or Ashley," she said, turning to face the two women, "but I think the receipt for the grapes that the sheriff found in Jessica's desk tells a different story."

"Probably planted," Mac said.

Now everyone's gazes were shifting between them.

Maris indicated the blonde teller. "Jessica would have been an easy target, especially considering her history with Edwin. If the murderer wanted a scapegoat, she was the perfect one."

"Wait a minute," Millicent said. "I don't understand one thing." She looked like she was on the edge of her seat. "What about the hit and run that put the doctor in a coma?"

"That's the thing," Maris answered. "The murderer would have needed access to Edwin's car."

Maris paused, looking at each of them. Kristofer's mustache looked as if it were twitching. Bryan had returned to looking at the ground. Millicent hadn't touched her crochet project for a number of minutes. Jessica looked like she might throw up, and Ashley looked like she was ready to burst.

"Only one person had access to everything that was needed for the crime," Maris said. She began to tick the items off on her fingers. "The grapes, the fresh seafood, the keys to the credit union—for planting the receipt in Jessica's desk and poisoning the grapes—and the keys to Edwin Martin's car." Slowly she turned to face Bryan. "The grapes disappeared after you arrived here, Bryan. You went into the kitchen to see your father, and you went by yourself. The doctor told you not to, but you didn't listen. Then you went to the bathroom, and you were in there for quite some time. At first I thought you were sick from seeing your dead father, but I think you were really disposing of the grapes. Did you flush them? Is that what happened?"

Millicent covered her mouth as she gasped, while Ashley and Jessica hugged each other. But all eyes, including Maris's were now focused on Bryan.

He raised his head and looked at her for a long time, not saying anything. Slowly, he crossed his arms in front of him and leaned back against the teller desk. If Maris didn't know she'd just accused him of killing his own father, she'd say he was contemplating a chess move.

"I guess this looks pretty bad for me, doesn't it?" he asked at last, his voice calm but no longer surprisingly so.

"Why did you do it, Bryan?" Maris asked.

He pushed away from the desk and

stepped closer to her. As she looked up at him, she hadn't realized he was so tall. As Bryan stared down at her, Maris saw Mac stiffen out of the corner of her eye.

"What do you want me to say?" the young man demanded. "That my dad was a cheapskate? That he cared about turning a profit more than his own son? Do you want me to tell you about how he starved me when I was a kid so I could 'learn the value of money,' or how I'm drowning in student debt because he refused to help me pay for school?" His reddening face twisted into a defiant glare. "Or what about how he kicked me out of the house, calling me a freeloader? Is that what you want to hear?" His hands bunched into fists at his sides, but his feet didn't move.

For a moment Maris caught a glimpse of a scared little boy and the father who didn't give a fig for him. He glowered at all of them, turning in a slow circle. It was as if he was challenging them to say what he did was wrong.

None of them did.

"How cruel are the parents," Mac said quietly, "who riches only prize." Whether it was Robert Burns or Tom Hanks, it was incredibly appropriate, given the situation.

Millicent set her crochet project on Edwin's desk. "Terrible," she muttered. "Just terrible."

Bryan turned to her, jutting out his chin.

"Not this," Millicent quickly added. "I mean that oxygen was too good for Edwin Martin, and I think we can all agree on that."

"I'd still have my family's business," Kristofer said quietly.

"But," Ashley said, tentatively, "what about Dr. Rossi?" She looked from Mac to Maris. "Who would want to kill him?"

Maris fixed her gaze on Bryan again. "I'm sure you remember that day in the market when you cut your hand," she said. "Dr. Rossi said he had something important to tell us about your father. I think he was planning to reveal the truth about his seafood allergy. You dropped the pickle jar as a diversion. In fact, you were willing to cut your own hand to keep him from talking."

Nostrils flaring and jaw muscles working, Bryan said, "Even if this all was true—which I'm not saying it is—you have no proof, Ms.

Seaver, only accusations and theories." His voice was chillingly calm.

Millicent made a little "hmph" noise, but said nothing more.

Mac gripped his utility belt and widened his stance. "I'm afraid that's not true. Dr. Rossi has regained consciousness. He's identified you as the driver in the hit and run, Bryan."

The young man's expression fell, but he said nothing.

"Bryan Martin," Mac said, moving slowly across the room to him, "I am placing you under arrest for felony hit and run." He reached behind him and brought out handcuffs.

For a moment Maris wondered if Bryan was going to fight, or maybe make a break for it, but he seemed to deflate, even as she watched. As Mac recited his rights, the young man obliged by moving his hands behind his back. But when Mac was done, Bryan stared at Maris.

"A hit and run carries a maximum prison sentence of four years," Bryan said slowly and deliberately, "and a maximum fine of ten thousand dollars." His composure was unnerving. "That's all I have to say."

Mac nodded to Maris, who said, "Thank you for coming, everyone. I think we're done."

For a few seconds, no one moved but then Mac slowly ushered Bryan to the door. The young man was back to simply staring at the floor, but as they passed her, Mac smiled and simply said, "Good work."

Slowly the others began to file out as well.

"I hope," Kristofer said, "that they send him to a low-security prison, the kind with windows. Because I'll visit him and cut the glass myself. Poor kid." Shaking his head, he gave Maris a long look. "I have a glazing job I need to get to. I'll see you back at the lighthouse, Maris."

"See you later, Kristofer," Maris replied. "I'll be home before too long."

As she watched him go, she saw Mac putting Bryan in the back seat of the SUV. He reached across him and buckled the seat belt.

"I can't believe this," said a voice at Maris's shoulder. She turned to see Jessica, who'd regained some color and stopped biting her nails. The tension seemed to have drained from her but been replaced by exhaustion. "I take it this means I'm free to go?"

Maris smiled at her. "Yes. I'm sure you are."

Jessica exhaled and let her hands drop to her sides. "It's over. I really thought they were going to put me away for it." She looked into Maris's eyes. "Thank you."

Maris touched her shoulder. "I'm glad I could help."

For the first time since Maris had initially come to the credit union, Jessica actually smiled. "Before we re-open, I think I'll make a cup of tea." She turned to go, but paused. "And I am never buying grapes ever again."

Mac started up the SUV, but paused to give Maris a wave before he drove away. *Good work*, he'd said. She smiled as she turned back to the credit union. It *did* feel like good work. Bear had been right. Doing the right thing was always the right thing to do.

Carrying her satchel of crocheting supplies, Millicent nearly trotted through the front door. "No time to waste," she said to Maris, her gray curls bobbing. "The ladies will want to know every detail." She waved goodbye without looking back. "Come crochet with us any time," she said over her shoulder.

That left Maris on the porch with Ashley. For a moment, neither of them spoke, simply looking after Millicent as she passed the red gazebo.

The young teller pushed her glasses up her nose. "The credit union board has made me the interim manager," she said.

"Good for you," Maris said. "Well deserved, if I may say so." Maris regarded the young woman. "Planning any changes?"

Ashley shook her head. "It's just an interim thing, so I won't have any real authority. But I think I'll dig into the records a bit and see about Dr. Rossi's house and Kristofer's family shop. Something there smacks of dubious business practices. At the very least, the board will want to know and there might be an opportunity for some form of restitution."

"Well," Maris said, "it sounds like you'll be busy." She paused and looked over Ashley's shoulder into the building. "But not too busy I hope." Ashley eyed her for a moment. "Because I still need to open an account."

28

The sun had nearly settled to the horizon by the time Maris returned to the B&B. The Longacre family had just left for an early dinner. It seemed Kristofer was still out on his job, since his truck wasn't out front. That left Maris with a bit of time before the Wine Down. She found Cookie in the living room, the fire already going, a book in her hands, and a cup of tea at her side.

Cookie looked up and took off her glasses. "How'd it go?"

"Pretty much as expected," Maris said, taking a seat. "I'm sure Bryan Martin killed his father, but he's been arrested for the hit and run that put Dr. Rossi in the hospital."

The chef frowned a bit. "I'm afraid you're going to have to explain that."

Maris recounted everything that had happened at the credit union. She finished with, "So Jessica's been released, Ashley's in charge, and I even opened an account."

"Millicent must have been over the moon with the whole thing," Cookie said.

Maris laughed a little, looking over at the fire when an ember popped. "Over Jupiter, more like." She watched the flames for a moment, remembering the older woman's ecstatic smile.

"Glenda would have been proud of you," Cookie said.

Maris blinked at the sudden pronouncement and then looked at Cookie and grinned. "Do you really think so? I mean, after all, I'm the lightkeeper, not a police officer."

"Nonsense," Cookie said, picking up her book. "What is a lightkeeper, after all? You tend and care for the lighthouse. In turn, it looks out for those in trouble." She put her glasses back on. "I'd say you were doing exactly what you needed to be doing. She'd be proud." With that, she went back to her book.

Of all the things that Maris had expected

from helping to solve the murder, feeling warm and fuzzy wasn't one of them—but she'd take it. She got up and headed in the direction of the kitchen to start thinking about the cheeseboard and wine. But a telltale, harmonica-like meowing drew her attention to the floor.

Mojo stood there, looking up at her with his big orange eyes. But when she stooped down to pick him up, he bounced away down the hallway. He paused, looked over his shoulder at her, and meowed again.

Maris grinned at the little cat. She still had plenty of time before she needed to start the cheeseboard, so she followed him. He went all the way back to her room, through it, and pawed the utility room door.

"I'll open it," she told him sternly. "But we are not going into that basement."

Then, to her surprise when she opened the door, he bounded right across the narrow room to the doorway that led to the lighthouse tower. He pawed that one too.

"You want to visit Claribel?" she asked, opening that door as well.

He trotted through, went directly to the first stair, and jumped up to it. As Maris approached him, he sat down but looked up the spiral staircase.

"Oh," she said, hands on hips. "So you don't want to be picked up in the house, but now that we're out here, you won't climb up."

He gave his signature meow.

Although she shook her head, she scooped him up. "I don't know why I'm doing this," she muttered. But she was immediately rewarded with a soft purr.

At the top of the tower, the evening was clear and gorgeous. The amber ball of the sun had begun to flatten against the skyline. Claribel's beam circled slowly above, as it always had. But to Maris's eyes, it seemed to sparkle brighter today. When Mojo squirmed and she let him down, she suddenly remembered his moment on the ouija board. He'd pushed the planchette over the sun symbol.

"Did you mean 'son' as in Bryan?" she asked him, hardly believing she was saying it out loud.

Although he ignored her as he sat and licked his front paw, her mind flashed back to him picking a tarot card as well. She and Cookie had looked at it.

"The one with the moon and crayfish,"

she muttered in amazement. Had that been an allusion to the shellfish allergy? There was no way Maris could be sure, but she resolved to take more interest in Mojo's talent with magical objects.

The sound of a horn giving three short toots drew her attention back to the water. *Seas the Day* was passing by, Slick returning after a day of fishing. She gave the old man's silhouette a wave, smiling even though he couldn't see her. He'd told her to follow her heading and it'd lead her to the truth. But what it'd really led her to was a new life and a sense of belonging in it.

"You know, Mojo," she said, stooping and picking him up. She ran her fingers through the soft hair between his ears. "I think I'm going to like this lightkeeper's gig."

As if in answer, he nuzzled her hand and gave her a tiny, tinny meow.

Another Pixie Point Bay book awaits you in The Witch Who Saw A Star (Pixie Point Bay Book 2).

For a sneak peek, turn the page.

The Witch Who Saw A Star

Excerpt

CHAPTER ONE

Maris Seaver looked at her watch and frowned. Despite the fog that surrounded the optics room of the lighthouse, she had expected to hear Slick's boat as he went by. Yet, at the appointed time when the three short toots of the horn would have sounded, she had heard nothing.

Could I have missed him?

Slick and *Seas the Day*, his commercial fishing boat, were as punctual as Big Ben and as consistent as the rise of the sun. Nor did the fog deter him. Water was second-nature to the elderly mariner. He'd been boating in Pixie Point Bay, and the ocean beyond, for decades. Although the Old Girl's beam was circling up above as it always did, Maris knew he didn't need it.

She brought the watch to her ear—it was ticking. Once again she peered out into the soupy white mist but the view of the bay was completely obscured. Only the lighthouse's small dock and the rocks directly below were visible.

I must have missed him.

As she checked the time yet again, she realized how late the hour was becoming. She had a B&B to run, and it was time—past time—to get back to it. With a sigh, she reluctantly turned away from the bay.

But as she passed the fresnel lens, she gave its base a gentle pat and said, "Keep an eye out for him, Claribel." If anyone could, it was the magical lighthouse.

Maris made her way down the spiral metal staircase and exited the conical white tower, choosing to walk down the side of the two-story Victorian home. The cool and salty mist enveloped her, and she could hear the waves on the rocks below the point. She mounted the steps to the back porch, passed through its vestibule and the front rooms, and followed her nose.

"What smells like heaven?" Maris asked, as she entered the kitchen. Cookie was at the stove.

"Just a little something I whipped up," Cookie said, with a smile. She eyed Maris's skirt and heels. "That's a pretty combination."

Like her Aunt Glenda, Maris favored skirts, low heels, and frilly blouses. Today she was dressed in a cornflower blue layered skirt, matching open-toed shoes, and a ruffled white blouse.

Ruth "Cookie" Calderon was wearing a short-sleeved cotton dress with her usual large, bright floral print, though it was mostly covered with an apron.

"Thank you," Maris said. "And you're looking your usual vibrant self." She looked over the smaller woman's shoulder. French toast was turning a golden brown in one of the skillets and she could see that Cookie was using her own homemade Italian panettone as the bread. "Genius," Maris said, her mouth watering at the wonderfully sweet scent. "What can I do to help?"

Though Maris wasn't sure, she thought Cookie hesitated.

After twenty-five grinding years in the hospitality industry, Maris pitched in wherever she could at the B&B, almost out of habit. But she also didn't want the seventy year old chef overdoing it. With shoulder length, salt and pepper hair that was more salt than pepper these days, Cookie had been at the B&B with Maris's aunt for decades.

"Eggs, sunny side up, are on the menu today," the older woman said. "And sliced almond bread for toast."

"I'm on it," Maris said.

She took one of the skillets standing by, lit a burner for it, and set it in place. After she added the butter, she went to the egg basket and fetched three fresh eggs. As she waited for the butter to melt, she unwrapped the loaf of almond bread.

Seeing that the butter was beginning to sizzle, Maris turned down the heat, picked up an egg and cracked it on the edge of the iron skillet. But as she opened it over the pan, a tiny bit of shell fell with the raw egg.

"*Rats*," she said, looking around for something to fetch it out. She spotted the butter knife. But the shell was under the egg white, which was already cooking. As she tried to scrape it to the edge, she accidentally hit the yolk, which began to run. "*Rats*."

"Over hard," Cookie said calmly. "I like eggs that way as well."

Maris looked at her, and Cookie must have realized she didn't understand. With a deft movement, she used the spatula already in her hand and flipped the egg over. Now the shell was on top. She held her hand out for the butter knife, and used it to flick the bit of shell onto the counter.

"Never crack an egg on the edge of the pan or a bowl," she said quietly, as she picked one up. "You basically force the broken shell up into the egg." She held it over the cutting board on the counter. "Always on the side, against something flat." Using just one hand, she cracked it, took it to the pan, and opened it. A perfectly whole yolk landed in the middle of the white, without a trace of shell. By now the first egg was done, and Cookie moved that to a waiting plate. She smiled at Maris. "Your turn."

But no matter how hard she tried, Maris simply couldn't keep from breaking the yolk: they caught on the shell; the yolk landed too hard; she even dropped the broken shell halves on top of one. She eyed the egg basket and how many were left.

"Shall I finish that?" Cookie asked, apparently seeing the same thing.

By the time Maris looked up from her collection of ruined eggs, the French toast and hash browns were in their warming trays—all done. Maris blinked at them.

Cookie moved the egg skillet to her side of the stove. "The warming trays are ready if you want to take those out."

It was time to admit defeat. "I'd be glad to," Maris said, which was completely true.

One by one she took them to the dining room, then the maple syrup, and the freshly squeezed orange juice in its pretty glass decanter. Back in the kitchen she filled the carafe with fresh coffee, brought it to the sideboard, and made sure the hot water dispenser was hot.

When she returned to the kitchen to wait for the eggs, she said, "By the way, I didn't hear Slick this morning. I'm sure I'm just a worrywart, and he's just taking a day off, but I thought it was strange."

Cookie snorted. "Slick doesn't take days off. He lives to fish, and he knows that most of the restaurants in Pixie Point Bay rely on him for their fresh seafood. More than a few places would be hard pressed to serve meals if he decided to take a few 'days off'."

Hard pressed to serve meals? It wasn't like Cookie to exaggerate, but did Slick really bring in that much fresh catch?

"Whatever the reason, I didn't hear him today." She shook her head and grimaced a little. "Hopefully he came by earlier or later than usual."

Cookie took two china teacups from the cupboard. "How about some tea?" the chef asked.

Although Maris's magic gift, like her aunt's, was precognition, Cookie's was making potions. If she made tea, you could rest assured it was just what you needed.

Maris smiled at her. "Do you have an anti-worrywart tea?"

Cookie gave her a mischievous grin. "I might. We can have it with our eggs." As she steeped their tea in a lovely china pot decorated with bouquets, she said, "I checked the cheeses so I could include some in tomorrow's breakfast, but we might be running a bit low."

Maris went to the stainless steel, double door fridge, and pulled out one of the clear drawers. "We could definitely do with a run to Cheeseman Village," she agreed. "I'll do that today."

The B&B's landline telephone rang just then, making both Maris and Cookie look at the time on the microwave. It was a bit early to call for a reservation but, then again, sometimes people called from faraway time zones. Maris went to the library and picked up the handset of the antique rotary phone.

"Pixie Point Bay Lighthouse and B&B," she said pleasantly. "How can I help you?"

"By coming to the pier," a familiar voice said.

"Slick?" Maris exclaimed. "Is that you? Are you all right?"

Cookie stood at the entry to the library and they exchanged worried looks.

"I'm fine," he said, and Maris let the breath she'd been holding go. She gave

Cookie the okay sign, who put a hand over her heart and smiled.

"When I didn't hear your horn this morning," Maris said, "I started to worry."

"You can still worry," Slick replied. "I'm afraid I need a favor."

Maris's eyebrows drew together. "Anything," she said. "Just name it.

"I wonder if you could come to the pier."

"The pier?" Maris looked over at Cookie, who was vigorously nodding and shooing her with one hand. "Of course. I can leave right now. Can you tell me what this is about?"

Slick was silent for a few moments before he said, "There's been a murder." He paused again. "On my boat."

• • • • •

Buy The Witch Who Saw A Star

FREE BOOK

If you'd like to learn how Maris arrived in Pixie Point Bay and got her start, you can read *The Witch Who Saw the Light* for FREE by signing up for my newsletter at the link below.

Get A Free Book

DEDICATION

For Mr. Bee's Knees

COPYRIGHT

Copyright © 2020 Emma Belmont

This is a work of fiction. Names, characters, places, and incidents are products of the author's imagination or are used fictitiously and are not to be construed as real. Any resemblance to actual events, locales, organizations, or persons, living or dead, is coincidental.

All rights reserved. No part of this book may be used or reproduced in any manner, stored in or introduced into a retrieval system, or transmitted, in any form, or by any means (electronic, mechanical, photocopying, recording, or otherwise), without the prior written consent of the copyright owner.

The scanning, uploading, and distribution of this book via the Internet or via any other means without the permission of the copyright owner is illegal. Please purchase only authorized electronic editions, and do not participate in or encourage electronic piracy of copyrighted materials. Your support of the author's rights is appreciated.